Also by Les Savage, Jr.
in Large Print:

The Bloody Quarter
Fire Dance at Spider Rock
Medicine Wheel
Phantoms of the Night
Coffin Gap
Table Rock
Treasure of the Brasada

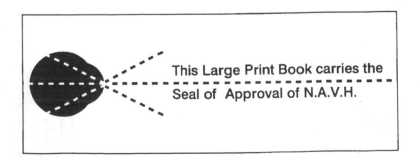

This Large Print Book carries the
Seal of Approval of N.A.V.H.

LAST
of the
BREED

Les Savage, Jr.

G.K. Hall & Co. • Thorndike, Maine

A short version of this novel was published in Zane Grey's Western Magazine under the title *Arizona Showdown*, copyright, 1951, by Les Savage, Jr.

Published in 2001 by arrangement with Golden West Literary Agency.

G.K. Hall Large Print Paperback Series.

The text of this Large Print edition is unabridged.
Other aspects of the book may vary from the original edition.

Set in 16 pt. Plantin by Warren S. Doersam.

Printed in the United States on permanent paper.

Library of Congress Cataloging-in-Publication Data

Savage, Les.
    Last of the breed / by Les Savage, Jr.
      p. cm.
    ISBN 0-7838-9342-6 (lg. print : sc : alk. paper)
    1. Fathers and sons — Fiction. 2. Arizona — Fiction. 3. Large
type books. I. Title.
PS3569.A826 L42 2001
   813'.54—dc21   00-053837

LAST
of the
BREED

1

The three of them rode through the purple dusk, through the juniper that grew thick and matted as a beard on the land, and came to a halt at the tip of the mesa. They were on the edge of the Rim country now and they could look southward for uncounted miles to where the shape of the Arizona desert died in the coming night. Tiger Sheridan spoke finally, in a voice husky with exhaustion.

"I hope there's bigger timber ahead. This scrub stuff ain't tall enough to hang a man on."

Brian Sheridan did not answer his father. He slackened in the saddle, trying to ease aching muscles, and with his bandanna wiped futilely at the grit masking his face. It was a bony face, with all the irrepressible humor of the Red Irish in its mobile lips and all their volatile temper in its blue eyes. That temper was boiling in him now. It had been a helluva long ride for nothing.

Indifferently he watched Robles dismount and begin hunting for tracks. Robles was a very old Apache, none knew exactly how old. He had ridden with Mangas Coloradas and Geronimo and had been one of the warriors who buried Cochise in Stronghold Canyon and who rode their horses through the gorge from dusk to dawn till every trace of the grave was obliterated. The strange hush hanging over the land made him nervous and he kept glancing apprehensively around and touching his medicine bag.

"Any fresh signs?" Brian asked.

"Old sign," Robles said. His voice was like the rustle of dry leaves. "Bad sign."

Brian turned to Tiger. "You sure you read those signals right?"

Tiger snorted. "I can read smoke signals good as any Indian. That was talk them Apaches were makin' on the reservation yesterday. Two hundred cattle and three men, they said. Traveling south and due to reach the Rim by sundown today."

Tiger's saddle squawked as he shifted his bulk impatiently. In any other age this man would have been a king. There was conquest in his face. Glacial eyes peered fiercely from beneath shaggy white brows and his nose was crooked and questing as an eagle's beak. But he was an old king now. His head was shaggy and white and bowed. A paunch sagged heavily against his belt and his ague kept him rubbing peevishly at massive joints.

"Your eyes goin' bad, old man?" he asked Robles. "If they went off the Rim they must of done it here." He jerked his leonine head at Brian. "Git down and have a look."

Robles stood to his full height, like a dog with his hackles up at the offense. Tiger took no notice. Robles had started working for him before Brian was born, and the two were like a pair of crotchety old sourdoughs constantly snapping at each other.

Brian dismounted stiffly and roamed through the juniper, bending low to study the ground in the strange twilight. He was six feet tall, long-legged, cat-flanked, his broad shoulders bowed now with the weariness of the long ride. Dust was caked all over him; it turned his Levis white, lay in chalky patches on his denim jacket, sparkled like frost on his days growth of red beard. Despite his exhaustion and disgust he had a streak of wry humor that would never allow him to take himself or his job too seriously. What if the cattle had been taken? It was just another of the minor rustlings that had been going on for years and would always plague an outfit the size of the Sheridan's vast Double Bit —

His rambling thoughts broke off sharply as he saw freshly turned earth and a broken branch. He almost dropped to one knee, then checked himself. He hated to shame Robles by succeeding where the old Apache had failed. He sought vainly for some way to help Robles save face in front of Tiger.

Then the desire left him as he realized this was ground Robles had already passed over. The Indian's eyes couldn't be that bad. Had he deliberately ignored the sign?

"You got something?" Tiger asked.

Brian glanced at Robles. Framed in a coarse mane of white hair, the Indian's face was an idol's mask of shimmering ridges and gaunt hollows, turned dark by the tobacco-stain of time and weather and age. It told Brian nothing.

"Looks like a lot of cattle," Brian said, dropping to one knee and studying the tracks. "Shod horses. Pretty fresh."

As Brian walked back to his horse, Tiger said, "This is what you been needing. I hope they put up a fight."

"I'll put the notches on my gun," Brian said.

Tiger slapped his saddle so hard the horse jumped. "Don't be so damn uppity. This is all part of the business. It's time you quit wenchin' and drinkin' and raisin' hell and got down to learnin' your trade."

Brian looked sullenly at him. "Who taught me to drink and raise hell?"

"That's different." Tiger scowled and tugged his longhorn mustaches uncomfortably. "Man gits old he's entitled to a little carousin'. What else has he worked for all his life? When I was your age I was workin' eighteen hours a day and didn't have a cent to spend come Saturday."

Brian gigged his Steeldust forward. It was the old bone of contention between them and he had heard the lecture a hundred times before. Hell, what did the old man expect of him? He'd lived all his life in the shadow of the great Tiger Sheridan. Every time he'd tried to learn the business or do something on the Double Bit it had ended up with Tiger taking the reins away from him.

Robles passed Brian, taking the lead. The Indian wore a purple cotton shirt frayed at the elbows and cuffs, and on his skinny legs was a pair of rawhide *chivarras* mottled with grease and desert dust. He did not look at Brian but in the compressed shape of his lips was his old disapproval of the younger man. Brian had never measured up to his conception of manhood.

Twilight seemed to flow away from them into darkness as they started the long drop. The Rim here was not a sheer cliff as it was farther west. It dropped down in talus slopes and slanting shelves, broken buttes and winding ridges that formed a gradual, tumbling descent for many miles until it reached the desert floor.

They crossed a long and twisted valley choked with scrub growth; they fought their way through clawing mesquite and stunted juniper and reached a cut that sliced its way through the transverse ridge forming the lower wall of the valley. The cut opened into a long park where a last stand of high country timber reached up to the sky. Brian sensed Tiger's head turn to look at it. They passed the timber and came to the edge of a slanting mesa and heard cattle lowing in the black pockets below them. Robles got off his horse and disappeared like a ghost in the darkness and Tiger and Brian sat their weary animals in silence for what seemed a lifetime. The tension built in Brian till it lay against him like an overwhelming pressure. Then Robles returned and walked to his horse; he put a hand on the saddle and looked back in the direction he had come.

"Well?" Tiger said.

"Our cattle," Robles said. "Circle rider hold them. Two men sleep in camp. No guard."

"We can ride right in," Tiger said.

Robles shook his head. "Better wait for daylight. Bad sign."

"What sign?"

"Why no guard? Maybe a trap."

"Trap, hell! They're just so damn played out they're mount up and take that circle gettin' careless. Now you mount up and take that circle rider. Brian and me'll hit camp."

The Apache was reluctant and hesitated a long time; finally he put his horse on the downslope again and angled off into the night. Tiger eased his saddle gun from its boot. All his hands carried Winchesters but he still clung to the old Spencer breechloader he'd used in the early days. Brian slipped his own .45/70 out of the scabbard.

"What's the matter with Robles?" he asked.

"He's just gettin' senile," Tiger said. "Now let's go."

They pushed their horses slowly off onto the trail that ran in tortuous switchbacks down the face of the crumbling rock. They reached the bottom of the pocket and saw the smoky movement of cattle in the matted growth ahead. The moon was up on their left now and in the silvery gloom they could see the shape of the camp.

Either these were men made careless by exhaustion or made reckless by the years they had been doing this without retaliation. For, like a horse switching its tail at flies, Tiger had tolerated the penny-ante rustlers hopping the border to cut out their handfuls of his beef.

A picketed horse snorted ahead of Brian and spooked away from him. It reached the end of its rope and brought up with a sharp squeal. Tiger's command came sharp and clear.

"Now."

They both touched spurs to their horses and rode hard into camp. Brian had a dim sense of two shapes rolling from their blankets and coming to their feet.

"Nacho?" somebody shouted.

Then Brian saw a smoky figure almost directly before him, running across in front of his horse. Tiger saw him too and yelled:

"Get him, Brian. Cut him down."

It was almost pointblank range and Brian could hardly have missed. Instead of firing he wheeled his horse into the man; its shoulder struck him a heavy blow on the chest and he went down. At the same time Brian heard the other man shout again, frantically:

"Don't shoot, you got me, you got me —"

Brian wheeled his horse and saw that Tiger had halted across camp, holding his gun on the man. Brian recognized him as Ramsey, a shift-less, wedge-faced idler who spent most of his time cadging drinks in Apache Wells. Brian's man was rolling over now, getting dazedly to his feet. The pale moonlight revealed him as another habitué of the Apache Wells saloons, the half-breed they called Nacho. He had a narrow, sun-blackened face, Aztec cheekbones, eyes that glittered green as a cat's in the treacherous moonlight.

"What the hell?" he said. "Where's Latigo?"

"What's Latigo got to do with it?" Tiger asked.

Robles trotted in, kicking up sand. "Circle rider got away," he said.

Tiger spat angrily and then glanced back at the pines. "Get a pair of ropes. Sling 'em over a high branch."

There were two horses picketed beside camp, still saddled, hipshot and briny with dried lather. As Robles turned his roan to get the dally ropes off their rigging, Nacho made a bleating sound.

"Tiger, you're makin' a mistake. We didn't take this herd. We're workin' for Latigo —"

"My foreman wouldn't make no deals with trash like you," Tiger said.

"He did, he did. He promised us a dollar a head for every beef we brought back. We come up with some long riders pushing this stuff across the Little Colorado."

"What long riders?"

"It was night. We couldn't see 'em. We had to fight for it."

14

"It's the truth," Ramsey said. "I swear it."

"I believe you," Tiger said caustically. He put his hands on the saddle horn and leaned forward. "I've taken all I'm goin' to, Nacho. When it was a dozen head at a time I let it go. I couldn't waste all my men chasin' every border hopper that came up from Sonora. But now you're gettin' too big for your britches. I'm gonna make an example of you. By tomorrow evenin' every man from here to the border will know what happens to the man who takes a Double Bit steer. That's the way it used to be and that's the way it's gonna be again." Tiger turned to Brian. "Get some tie-ropes and lace 'em up."

Brian saw the wicked gleam in Tiger's eye. The old man was just putting the fear of hell in these men. He couldn't be serious about hanging them.

Brian played along, dismounting and walking to the heap of gear by the dead ashes of the fire. He found some short piggin' strings on a pack saddle and took a pair of them. Nacho had begun pleading again but Tiger was not listening. A little muscle began to twitch in Ramsey's cheek and he was death-pale.

While Tiger held the rifle on them Brian tied their hands behind their backs. Ramsey submitted, trembling now. Nacho started to fight, refusing to put his hands at his back. Tiger cocked the Spencer, Nacho stopped struggling, glaring at the old man.

When Brian had finished, he helped the two

15

onto their saddled horses. All the way up the switchbacks Nacho alternately pleaded with Tiger and cursed him foully. Robles had made the two dally ropes fast to the trunk of a tree, then had slung them over a high branch. Tiger halted beside the dangling nooses and nodded at the Apache. Stony-faced, the Indian slipped the first noose over Ramsey's head. The slat-limbed puncher began to writhe from side to side like some animal in a trap, spittle becoming foam at the edge of his lips. A frantic note made Nacho's voice shrill.

"Tiger, damn you, at least give us a chance. Go get Latigo. He hired us, I tell you —"

Robles slipped the noose over Nacho's head. Brian looked at the deep grooves in his father's face and began to stir uncomfortably. He pulled his horse close and spoke in a low voice.

"Hasn't it gone far enough? You couldn't scare them much more?"

Surprise widened Tiger's eyes. Then he shook his massive head in disgust. "What kind of milk sop have I got for a son? I guess that's the trouble with this whole country. There hasn't been a decent hangin' around here in so long we're all goin' soft." He turned to Robles. "Slap those horses on the rump."

Realization hit Brian like a blow. This was a part of the Tiger Sheridan legend — a part of the fire and brimstone, the savage violence and primitive code that had allowed the man to carve an empire out of the Indian-infested wilderness.

But most of that legend had been created while Brian was too young to take part in it, so that the incredible feats and conquests had become as much myth as reality to him. In these last years Tiger had been an aging, arrogant old man, living in the reflected aura of past glories. Maybe he'd once been as great as everybody said but not to his own son. . . .

As Robles edged his roan toward the noosed men, Brian kicked his Steeldust into a run that took it between the Indian and the other pair. He reined it to a halt, facing Tiger.

"You can't do it this way. Maybe Nacho's telling the truth. You've got to give them a chance."

Tiger's face was blank for an instant. Then he made a savage sound. "Nacho's a born liar. Are you gonna git out or am I gonna shoot you out?"

There was a withering ferocity in his face, but Brian did not move. They faced each other in the intense silence.

When Tiger was finally convinced that Brian would not move, he shouted with rage and jerked the gun toward the ground. The shot made a deafening crash. All the horses jumped in startled fright and the animal beneath Nacho bolted.

The rope pulled Nacho off the horse's rump; his body jerked like a sack of meal and then swung wildly through the air. With an outraged shout Brian wheeled his Steeldust toward the man, snatching his Barlow knife from a hip pocket. The motion took the Steeldust across the front of Ramsey's horse. It had started to bolt also but the Steeldust jamming up against it stopped the animal before Ramsey was pulled off.

"Damn you," bawled Tiger, "let them be!"

But Nacho had swung back, crashing into the Steeldust. With his knife open, Brian slashed at the rope. Hemp parted, dropping the man heavily to the ground. At the same time Tiger began firing again.

The deafening crash and the bullets kicking up dirt around their feet made both Ramsey's horse and the Steeldust rear frantically. Brian felt himself going out of the saddle. He caught at the headstall of Ramsey's horse as he fell.

His weight pulled the animal's head almost down to the ground and he thought his arms would be jerked from their sockets. It was like bulldogging a steer. As Brian's boots struck the ground the horse tried to spin and bolt. The horse had to drag Brian's whole weight with him and though he managed to wheel in a half-circle, it kept the animal from running.

"Let him go," Tiger bawled. "I'll shoot your legs off."

He jammed a fresh shell into the old breechloader and fired again. Deafened by the crashing gun, with the slug kicking dirt against his legs, Brian hung onto the plunging horse. Ramsey had his legs clamped around the animal like a bronc peeler, his slack body jerked violently from side to side by the plunging beast.

Brian caught the bit, yanking down viciously. The horse squealed in pain and quit its wild rearing. In a fury, Tiger fired again at Brian, the bullet striking so close he could feel the jarring impact through his boot. But he turned in angry defiance toward his father, refusing to release the frantic horse. Jamming another shell into the breech, Tiger jerked the gun up till it covered Brian's chest. The old man's face was choleric and his whole body shook with fury. Brian could see his finger trembling against the trigger.

At last, however, he settled back into the saddle of his fiddling, excited horse. He glanced contemptuously at Nacho, who was groaning and trying to roll over. Brian knew a moment of relief that the man's neck hadn't been broken.

The rage left Tiger's face abruptly, and he let out an explosive laugh. He looked at Brian, with a frosty gleam in his eyes that could have been grudging pride.

"Dammit," he said, "maybe the cub has some starch in his backbone after all. Maybe."

2

Apache Wells was a desert town, lying on a flat table of land that ran twenty miles northward to the Rim and outward in every other direction beyond sight. From ten miles off the windows began flashing at a man like heliographs in the blinding sun. From half a mile away the buildings looked like toy playing-blocks strewn on the floor by a careless boy. The Salt River Trail came down off the Rim and became Cochise Street where it met the town, running four blocks between false fronts and wooden overhangs and sagging tie-racks. Alkali was everywhere, sifting up from beneath the traffic to hang in the air like a silken haze, powdering the rumps of horses at the racks, caking thick and white on the windows and walls of the buildings.

Brian and his father reached the town on Saturday morning. They had ridden the previous night out, coming down off the Rim, driving Nacho and Ramsey along with them. Tiger had meant to take them directly to the sheriff's office and swear out a warrant, but when he saw his foreman's big Choppo horse in front of the Black

Jack he pulled to a halt. Men began to gather immediately, hailing the two Sheridans and looking curiously at the prisoners.

Without offering explanation, Tiger sent Robles into the saloon after Latigo. In a few minutes the Double Bit foreman appeared. He was a tall, heavy-framed man in linsey-woolsey jeans and a buckskin shirt turned chalky by a week of roundup dust. He had a long bony jaw shadowed by a blue stubble of beard, and his heavy-lidded, indolent eyes were red-rimmed from the sleepless nights and driven labor of the past weeks.

"What the hell you doin' in town?" Tiger asked.

"Boys been three weeks without a letup," Latigo said. "I thought I'd give 'em a day off."

Tiger considered that, then glanced at Nacho. "We caught this man with two hundred Double Bit steers. He said you hired him to run 'em down."

Latigo looked at Nacho. The breed said thinly, "They wouldn't believe me. They was going to string me up."

"I offered Nacho a dollar a head for every steer he recovered," Latigo told Tiger.

It seemed to take all the wind out of Tiger. He settled in his saddle, glowering at Latigo. For a moment he was just an old man, exhausted and confused. Then he sent an oblique glance at Nacho, swearing softly. "What right've you got makin' deals with him?" he asked Latigo.

A rush of color dyed the foreman's bony cheeks. "What's wrong with Nacho? Seems like he got more cattle back in one haul than we've got all this year with the other ways you been trying."

Tiger shook his head. "Dammit, I wish you'd tell me these things before you let me go makin' a fool of myself." A deeper color crept into Latigo's face under the rebuke. Tiger jerked his hand angrily at the prisoners. "Give 'em back their hardware," he told Brian. He stepped off his horse, wheezing and grunting like an old bull. "I guess there's only one way to make it right. Let's all go have breakfast. If you want to git drunk after that, it's on the Double Bit."

His stubborn old pride wouldn't let him look at Nacho or Ramsey. Brian handed the breed back his six-shooter, speaking tiredly. "Tiger means you too. Give him a chance to unwind. This has made a fool of him."

Nacho looked at Tiger. He licked his lips and ran his thumb across one pock-marked cheek. Then he grinned, slowly and balefully. "Sure," he said. "Sure."

The whole crowd moved after Tiger into the Black Jack. Brian dismounted wearily and made his tie at the rack. He heard George Wolffe hail him and turned to see the man crossing the street. Wolffe handled all the Double Bit's business and had a successful practice in town, but he had never lost the painful conservatism molded into him by his hard youth. His broad, solid body was still clothed in a shabby black clawhammer coat and homespun jeans. In his black eyes was an unceasing watchfulness of life's minutest details and the caliper grooves on either side of his lips compressed them into chronic disapproval of any variation in the status quo.

Wolffe had been orphaned at fourteen, forced to work as a stable hand to support himself and his sister. At seventeen he had begun studying law at night and at twenty had passed the bar examination. He had gone into the office of Sam Root, Apache Wells's only other lawyer, and when Root had died a year ago, Wolffe had inherited all the legal business in town. George Wolffe wasn't much to look at, but he was a man who knew exactly what he was doing, and why.

He looked worriedly at the dust caked on Brian. "What happened now?" he asked.

Brian told him the story and Wolffe broke in with a surprised sound. "And you went with them?" he asked.

"I had to," Brian explained ruefully. "I was the only one around home besides Robles. Tiger read those smoke signals and got this thing in his craw and even Robles couldn't stop him with all that talk of bad sign on the range."

"I wouldn't laugh at Robles," Wolffe said. "Those Indians know things we don't. Personally I think there is something strange going on."

Brian chuckled. "What's the matter, George?

23

Price of feed go up two cents?"

"Don't joke, Brian. We got word another band of Apaches has jumped reservation and disappeared in the Superstitions. You don't find them that restless without good reason."

Brian glanced past Wolffe to the Superstitions, lying like pale blue ghosts on the horizon. They were the mountains of a hundred legends and a hundred lies. A dozen men had disappeared back there during Brian's lifetime, hunting the mythical Lost Dutchman or on the trail of marauding Apaches. When Geronimo had surrendered there were some among his renegades who could not be accounted for. It was said they had fled to the Superstitions and were being joined, year by year, by the other bronco Apaches who jumped reservation.

For a moment the sight of the mountains, cloaked in haze and seeming to float like a pale vapor on the horizon, touched something primitive in Brian. He recalled the strange hush on the Rim yesterday, and Robles's apprehension — and a hint of the old Indian's superstitious fears brushed him.

"It's funny," he said. "Robles didn't want Tiger to go after those cattle. He really didn't."

Wolffe grasped his arm. "That's what I mean, Brian. You shouldn't have let Tiger go. He's too old to do the things he used to. You've got to take some responsibility on your own shoulders."

Brian poked him affectionately in the ribs. "I

like you, George, but you should be an under-taker. Right now I feel too grimy to enjoy break-fast. How about a shave?"

Wolffe hesitated, then pulled a key from his pocket and gave it to Brian. "You know where the stuff is. And please don't leave lather in my mug."

Brian laughed and clapped him on the back and started across the street. Wolffe lived with his sister in rooms over the feed store. They were reached by a rickety outside stairway that led to a second floor landing.

The first room was Wolffe's office, containing a battered pigeon-hole desk and a pair of sagging leather chairs. Arleen Wolffe's frilly curtains and hooked rugs seemed a pitiful feminine attempt to cover the barren simplicity so characteristic of Wolffe.

Their bedrooms were more livable. In George's room Brian found the razor and soap and shaving mug in the precise place and the precise position he had found them a hundred other times after an all-night binge in town. He removed his shirt, filled a crockery bowl with water, and began lathering up. He was humming tunelessly to himself when the outer door opened.

"George?" It was Arleen's voice.

"Brian," he answered.

She came to the door, her arms full of gro-ceries. She was as Indian-dark as her brother, black-haired, black-eyed, with lips that bloomed like an exotic flower in the fragile oval of her face. A close-fitting basque coat outlined the supple lines of her body as far down as the waist; then they were lost in the flaring foam of lace and ruffles that formed her skirt.

She pouted wryly. "Winners?"

He began to shave. "No card game. I was out being responsible."

Her delicate black brows arched in surprise. "I can't believe it."

"Tiger and me. Hunting down rustlers. All day and all night. You'd have been proud of me."

"Did you catch them?"

"Strung 'em up."

"Brian, you didn't!"

He flipped soap into the bowl, chuckling. "Hardly. They turned out to be Latigo's men, bringing back some Double Bit stuff that had been run off."

Her lips grew petulant and she shook her head, sighing in disappointment. "You can't even do it when you try, can you?"

"Fate," he said. "I wasn't meant to be responsible."

She disappeared and he could hear the crackle of paper sacks as she put the groceries down in the kitchen. Then she was back, taking off her bonnet and shaking out her hair. She studied him a moment, soberly, then said:

"Brian, what do you want in life?"

"Wine, women, song."

"Really?"

He stopped shaving, looking at her in the mirror. He knew this was just another way of asking him when he was going to settle down. It seemed to come around to that with everybody, lately. And yet, somehow, the question stuck in his craw. He frowned at his reflection.

"I guess I hadn't thought much about it," he said.

"Think now."

"You sound like George."

"Are you afraid to face it?"

He grew impatient. "What should I want? I've got everything the rest of you scramble for."

A change came to her face; her eyes narrowed and her mouth grew fuller, almost pouting. Then she smiled. "You're right, Brian. I do sound like George."

She came to the stand, wet the towel in the basin, and washed the remains of the lather off his jaw. Standing this close, the perfumed sensuality of her body enveloped him. He felt a heated flush come to his face and the pulses began their warning thump at his temples.

He took the towel from her hands, dropping it on the stand, and reached for her. A tight shape came to her lips and she wheeled out of his arms, walking to the window. He started to follow her, then checked himself. They were on the edge of something foreign to their relationship. She had been one of the few who could take him as he was, who could laugh wholeheartedly at his escapades, who could accept whatever measure of

27

lighthearted and capricious romance he chose to give, without questioning or asking for more.

"No games?" he asked flippantly.

She tilted her head back, face drawn and pale about the mouth. Looking at the sky, through the window. Looking at nothing.

"Won't the day ever come when you want to get serious?" she asked.

He took his shirt off the chair and slipped into it. "You're in a strange mood today."

She did not answer. He finished buttoning his shirt. She turned, slowly. A change had gone through her again. The impudent look was on her face, the slow, knowing smile. Then she threw back her head and laughed. It was a rich, wild laugh, and with the loosened black hair cascading down her back and framing her face it made her look savage. For a moment it convinced him that she had been baiting him all along. He started toward her across the room.

"I should paddle you," he said.

She evaded him and ran into the office. He followed and she circled the desk, breathing heavily now, a flush on her laughing face. She evaded him again and ran across the room and stood with her back against the wall. He started to follow but her head came up and her whole body was stiff against the wall and though the flush of laughter still tinted her face there was a note to her voice that stopped him.

"Please, Brian. Not today."

He was held moveless by her strange mood.

This wasn't the Arleen he knew. She had always been able to play the game, laughingly, perhaps a little sardonically.

"What is it, Arleen?"

She looked at him a long time, searching for something, in him, perhaps in herself. "I don't know," she said.

Before he could speak again there was a tramping on the stairway outside and a pounding on the door. He turned and opened it to see Dee Hadley, the banker's kid, panting on the landing.

"Better come quick, Brian. Tiger's drunk and there's a big fight at the Black Jack."

Brian sent a helpless look at Arleen, then hurried past the boy and down the stairs. As he quartered across the street he could hear the sounds from a block away — the shouting, the crash of glass, the smashing of furniture. As he approached the saloon a man pitched through the open door and fell on his back, skidding into the street. Brian saw that it was Ramsey.

"What is it?" Brian called.

The man rolled over in the dust, shaking his head dazedly. "Tiger drank too much before eatin'. He's mad because we made such a fool of him."

Brian plunged into the saloon. It was a shambles. There were so many men fighting it was hard to tell who stood against whom. It was always this way with Tiger's brawls; his enormous animal explosions seemed to infect the

29

whole place. Charlie Casket, the house man for the Black Jack, was backed against the wall, defending himself with a chair against two Mexicans. Jigger, the keg-shaped little bartender, had jumped on top of the bar. Barefooted, with a bungstarter in each hand, he was running up and down and shouting and cracking any heads that came within range.

Brian jammed his way through the struggling mass, buffeted back and forth, dodging wild blows, Latigo had apparently been standing with Tiger at the far end of the room but somebody had downed the foreman and he huddled on hands and knees against the bar, spitting blood. Tiger was the center of a vortex in the corner. Three men were on him, slugging, kicking, trying to pull the old man down.

One of them was Nacho. A second was Wirt Peters, a small cattle operator from south of Apache Wells. The third was Cameron Gillette, eldest son of Pa Gillette, a dry farmer from the Salt River Valley. Brian saw Wirt Peters smash Tiger across the side of the head with a roundhouse that knocked the old man back against the wall. Tiger jackknifed one leg, planted his boot in Peters's middle, and drove him halfway across the room. But Nacho struck Tiger in the belly, swinging him around so that his back was to Cameron.

Cameron came in with his fist raised to sledge Tiger across the back of the neck. But Brian caught Cameron from the flank, swung him around, and drove a blow at his chin. Cameron was a heavy, plodding man, not quick enough to dodge. He took the blow full; his face went slack and he staggered backward and sat down.

At the same time Wirt Peters came back in. Feet stamping wide, arms crooked, he had all the momentum of a charging bull. His rush smashed Brian against the wall. Stunned, Brian tried to tear loose. Peters swung a blow that caught him on the side of the face.

For a moment Brian was blinded. He pawed for Peters's hair and got a hold, yanking the man's head down and bringing his own knee up. It struck flesh and bone with a sodden crack and Brian felt the man's weight fall away from him.

Vision was returning in bright speckled flashes and Brian saw that Cameron was on his feet again. Brian was sick from the blows and his legs were like water. He knew he was in no shape to meet Cameron.

As the man came at him, Brian pushed away from the wall, feinting him into a lunge, then swinging out of the way. The big man plunged helplessly past, going right into the wall. Before he could turn back, Brian caught up a chair, bringing it down across the man's head and shoulders with the last of his strength.

Cameron made a deep grunting sound and went to his knees against the wall. He remained that way with his head bent and his hands braced flat against the wall. He groaned and tried to rise. He got a few inches up the wall and then sank back.

Tiger stood five feet away, swaying above Nacho. The breed lay flat on his back, glassy-eyed and out cold. Red veins netted Tiger's eyes and his neck was swollen till it looked ready to burst.

"Come on," he roared. "I just got my second wind. Who says I ain't got the right to string up a rustler?"

But it was over as quickly as it had started. Those who hadn't been knocked down stood limp and winded in the wreckage, gaping foolishly around them. Brian dropped the chair he was holding.

Swaying, Tiger looked around at Cameron Gillette, still crouched dazedly against the wall — at Wirt Peters, sitting on the floor and holding a bloody face. Tiger's eyes swung to Brian, and there was a grudging pride in his broad grin.

For a moment Brian felt closer to the old man than he'd been in a long time. Why did it have to be this way? Why did it take a crazy, schoolboy thing like a saloon brawl to bring out their real affection for each other?

"Been a long time since we stood back to back in a fight," Tiger said.

Brian grinned weakly. "Oughtta do it more often."

Reaction was setting in now and he fought to keep from being sick. The old man was right. His night life had left him soft as dough. The fight hadn't lasted more than a minute after he joined it and here he was trembling like a schoolgirl. Tiger saw the foggy look to his eyes, the pinched expression around his lips. Some of the gruff pride left the old man's face. He caught hold of a chair and swung it away from the table for Brian.

"You better git back in training before we do it more often," he said.

Brian saw one of the watching men smirk. Resentfully he lowered himself into the chair. His moment of affinity with the old man was gone. He sucked in a shaking breath, watching Tiger get another chair and sprawl into it, boots thrust out in front of him.

"Jigger," he bawled.

The barefoot bartender picked his way through the overturned tables with a bottle and some glasses. "I'd like such a fight every day if somebody'd pay for the damage," he said.

Tiger waved his hand magnanimously. "Put it on the bill." Wirt Peters and Cameron Gillette were recovering now. Cameron got up and leaned against the wall, staring around blankly. "Wirt," Tiger said, "you're a prime brawler, but you can't use your feet. Wash your face off with this coffin varnish and then put some inside you."

Peters found a chair and hauled it to the table. There was no malice left in these men after one of Tiger's brawls. They had fought with him a dozen times before and rarely did one of them come out of it an enemy to the old man. Peters poured whisky in his hands, washed the blood off his face. Tiger poured drinks all around. Brian closed his eyes and downed it. Still weak and shaking from the violence, he was unprepared for the raw jolt of whisky. He choked and coughed and had to spew up half the drink.

"Take it easy, boy," Tiger said. "You don't have to keep provin' you're a man."

The patronizing tone in his voice deepened Brian's resentment. Why had he even bothered defending the old man? Brian saw that Nacho was beginning to revive and he looked defiantly at Tiger.

"Tell me just one thing," Brian said. "Were you really going to hang them?"

Tiger gaped at Brian. Then he threw his head back and let out a deafening bray of laughter. "Son," he roared, "when in hell are you gonna grow up? If I thought it would dry you out behind the ears, I'd take 'em back there right now and string 'em up for you."

Brian flushed and hauled himself out of the chair. "If I stick in your craw that much you can finish your next brawl by yourself."

Then he turned and walked out.

3

Forty years ago Tiger Sheridan had driven his first herd cattle to the edge of the Rim country and had started the Double Bit. His house had been an adobe *jacal,* growing a room a year, according to Tiger's proud boast, until it comprised forty rooms, sprawled out through the sage and the matted juniper in baronial splendor. There was a living-room forty feet long with a flagstone fireplace at each end, a pine-floored dining-room that would seat a hundred guests, countless patios cupped within the walls of surrounding bedrooms and sitting-rooms.

Tiger's bedroom was famous throughout the land. Second only to the living-room in size, it was a chamber reflecting the crude, barbaric tastes of a man whose life had been devoted to founding a wilderness empire. The savage color of Navajo blankets covered the adobe floor; the furniture was a hopeless welter of colonial Spain and New England. Spool-turned settees stood beside leather-covered chests brought up the Turquoise Trail two hundred years ago. And in the very center of the great room was the incredible brass bed Tiger claimed he had gotten from Manuel Armijo, the infamous governor of Santa Fe during its Mexican period.

At seven o'clock in the morning, two days after the fight in town, Brian tried to get past the door of that garish chamber and reach his own room beyond. He had taken his boots off so tinkling spurs would not betray him. But the door was ajar, and as he cat-footed past it a roar seemed to shake the whole house.

"Brian!"

He halted, grimacing to himself. Then he moved to the door and pushed it all the way open. Morning sunlight made a blinding shimmer against the brass bed and Brian squinted his eyes shut painfully. Within the travesty of velvet canopies and glittering posts and brazen whorls lay the old man. He was propped up on pillows and naked to the waist, grimacing and grumbling as Robles rubbed a mixture of hot arnica, neat's-foot oil, and gunpowder into the cuts and bruises he had garnered in the fight. Tiger scowled at the blue circles under Brian's eyes and the fuzz of red beard on his jaw.

"Stud?" he asked.

"Draw," Brian said.

"And a woman."

"Celia."

"That little tramp."

"You asked her mother to marry you."

"Forty years ago, after a six-day drunk, blind in one eye," Tiger said. He pushed Robles peevishly aside, threw back the covers, swung his feet onto the floor. He sat scowling at his crooked, horny toes, a big, surly grizzly of a man, with tufts of hair sprouting like gray weeds from his beefy shoulders. "You'll eat breakfast with me this morning," he said. "Then we'll go down to the corrals. They brought in some fresh broncs for the saddle strings. After that we'll go out to roundup —"

"Tiger," Brian groaned.

"Git your workin' clothes on," Tiger said. "If you're gonna play you gotta pay."

Robles stood behind Tiger like a dark statue. But Brian thought he caught a gleam of secret amusement in the old Indian's eyes. Brian's was bristling with anger as he went out into the hall. When would Tiger stop riding him? The old man caroused as much as he did, put in hardly any more work than he did. What right did he have to this constant nagging? The ranch practically ran itself. Whenever Brian did try to help he always ended up feeling futile, as useless as a fifth wheel.

He stripped to the waist and got out his shaving things, unable to put it out of his mind. It made him think of Arleen's strange mood the other day. Was she going to begin too? He didn't think he could stand that. And he didn't think he could put up with Tiger much longer either.

"Oh, hell!"

He had cut himself and he dabbed futilely at the blood. He shouldn't let it get under his skin like this. He tried to drive it from his mind as he finished shaving. He changed to jeans and Justins and left the room still dabbing at the cut. He was startled by Robles, standing outside the door. The old Indian's white mane shone like a halo in the gloomy hall.

"No let Tiger go to roundup," he said.

Brian frowned at him. "You been reading smoke signals again?"

"Bad sign," Robles said. He moved his hand northward. "Bad sign up there." He made a half circle with his hand. "All over."

Brian was too tired to humor the old man. "You know he's dead set on going out there today," Brian said. "I can't stop him."

He went down the hall and joined Tiger in the dining-room. The old man would have nothing but steak and apple pie for breakfast. Brian had half a pot of black coffee and listened with closed eyes while Tiger lectured him on his wayward life. After that, belching gustily, Tiger led him down to the corrals.

They covered the rolling land behind the house, some made of adobe walls, others of pine poles brought from heavy timber farther north. It had been a hard roundup and the saddle strings were suffering. In the unaccustomed heat so many horses had become wind broken and used up that Tiger had been forced to bring some fresh stock from his herds on the high range. Brian and his father strolled past a sprawling adobe pen filled with two dozen skittish broncs that hadn't yet been broken to the saddle. Beyond that was a pole pen where three men were sacking out a snaky roan. It had a gunny sack tied on its back and was bucking crazily around the corral. It was a mean-looking animal, big-chested, with heavy mountain muscle that bulged like fists in its rump at every leap.

Tiger leaned against the poles, squinting at the horse. "That an old brand on it, Kaibab?" he shouted.

One of the men turned, a lean and hungry-looking bronc stomper with a battered face and scarred hands. "You remember Snakebite, Mr. Sheridan. We caught him two years ago. We couldn't break him then and I don't think we can do it now."

"How can you tell?" Tiger said.

"We sacked him out all yesterday and it ain't taken him down a single notch."

"Then it's time to put a man on him," Tiger said. "I don't pay you to wear out my gunny sacks."

"He looks pretty mean," Brian said. "Better let 'em wear him down a little more."

"He's no meaner'n a hundred others broke in these pens," Tiger said. He raised his voice. "If you don't want to top him, Kaibab, I'll get the Barker kid."

Pride made a dark stain against Kaibab's battered face. Brian saw the twinkle in Tiger's eyes and realized he had used the threat deliberately. The stomper waved an arm at the horse and the two handlers shook their ropes out, worked him into a corner, and put their lines on him. Then they started him toward the chutes. He fought every inch of the way, lather furled on him in dirty yellow ropes. There was a look of unalloyed viciousness about the horse that curled Brian's guts. Its eyes were wild and bloodshot and its whinnies and squeals came in shrill, savage gusts.

They finally got it into the chute and dropped the saddle on. Kaibab glanced at Tiger, hitched his pants up, and climbed up the fence. With a foot on each fence, straddling the chute beneath, he looked down on the thousand pounds of battering, screaming fury penned in the narrow space beneath him. Then he spat, pulled his hat down tight, and nodded.

The handler swung open the door and Kaibab dropped into leather as the horse plunged out. It was the wildest show Brian had ever seen. The horse made noise all the time, screaming, wheezing, grunting, whinnying, squealing.

The dust boiled up so thick that Brian finally lost sight of them and didn't even see Kaibab go off. When the horse appeared again, still bucking, the saddle was empty.

The handlers ran for the animal with their ropes, blocking him off in a corner so he wouldn't trample Kaibab. In a moment Kaibab appeared, crawling from the clouds of dust on hands and knees. He was bleeding from the ears and nose and was so dazed that he didn't hear them call to him. Brian and Tiger ducked through the bars and ran to him, trying to help.

But the man wouldn't come off his hands and knees. All Brian could do was guide him to the bars. Here he sagged, retching feebly. Tiger got a dipper of water from the trough near by and brought it to him. The old man wet his bandanna and washed Kaibab's face off; then he tilted the dipper to his lips. The stomper drank a little, spewed out the rest. The glazed look was gone from his eyes. He looked up at Tiger, voice weak.

"I've seen a lot of ugly ones," he said. "You won't break that horse, Mr. Sheridan."

Tiger's face grew channeled with disgust. "You gettin' old, Kaibab? In my day we topped a horse till he was busted, or we turned in our time."

Kaibab got to his feet. "You giving me my choice?" he asked.

"I sure as hell am," Tiger said. "I don't want a man around that's lost his guts."

"That isn't fair, Dad," Brian said. "You know this animal's history. You haven't got any right to make a man ride an outlaw."

Tiger turned slowly to Brian. A bright little flame of anger began to glow in his sun-faded eyes. "I guess you really need to learn this business," he said. "Ain't you found out by now that

41

I never ask a man to do somethin' I wouldn't do?"

Without waiting for an answer he stooped through the fence, shouting at the handlers. "Git him back in the chute. This one's goin' to be topped."

Brian went after him. "Dad, don't be crazy. You can't take a pounding like that —"

Tiger's answer was to get a rope and stamp to the other side of the corral, helping the handlers to snare Snakebite. It was a titanic battle to get him to the chute. Tiger strained and swore and fought with the other two men, until the animal was in the narrow slot. Brian knew how useless it was to argue with the old man, but he grabbed Tiger's arm and tried to talk him out of it. His father shook him off and turned to climb the fence.

"Tiger, don't be a fool," Brian yelled. "Everybody knows there isn't a one in the rough string you can't top. You don't have to keep proving it till they break you up."

"Sure, Mr. Sheridan," Kaibab called. "Come on down. I'll top him again."

"Open that door," bawled Tiger.

Stubs, the handler at the door, hesitated, glancing at Brian as if for help. But Tiger towered above them like some bow-legged, big-bellied god, and the fierce look on his face told them he would tolerate no opposition to his will. Stubs had been obeying this man unquestioningly for twenty years and one glance up at that scowling face made him grab the rope that raised the door.

The horse came out like a jackrabbit. Tiger Sheridan's great weight dropping into the saddle drove a wheezing grunt from deep within the roan. Then the animal screamed and started fence worming. He shot into the air headed toward one corner of the pen and came back down faced toward another. The four legs drove into the earth like ramrods and the ground shook beneath Brian. He thought it would drive Tiger's spine through his hat every time they came down.

But Tiger was sticking. He lost his hat and his white mane flapped around his head like a banner. His ribald shouts mingled with the horse's wild squeals till it was hard to tell them apart.

"Come on, you shad-bellied crowbait, let's see some real steam. I rode ornerier snakes than you when I was in diapers. Come on, you slab-sided buzzard grub, let's see you pinwheel —"

And pinwheel he did. Spinning like a top, cutting the ground to ribbons, kicking up great furls of dust that billowed around them like red smoke. Half the time Brian could not see them. Half the time he could only hear Tiger's wild yelling and the roan's frustrated screams.

It was a battle between giants. None of the men could remain still and watch it. Brian ran up and down the fence, a coiled rope in one hand, so excited that he was shouting advice to Tiger now.

"Don't let 'im sunfish, Tiger, don't let him sunfish, keep him out of that corner, he'll wipe you off on the fence —"

The roan came charging out of the dust at the men and they had to scatter. He headed straight for the fence, show bucking and jackknifing, apparently so enraged that he meant to charge into the poles. Another rider, with that fence coming at him, might have taken a dive. Tiger stuck to the saddle, bawling at the horse and even spurring him on.

At the last moment, with a frustrated scream, the roan swapped ends. Tiger lost a stirrup and for a moment Brian thought he was gone. But he shifted his weight with a desperate heave and was still in the saddle as the horse started bucking in the other direction.

In a frenzy, the roan pulled the plug. Crawfish, double-shuffle, pump handle, they were all there, coming in such dizzying succession that it was impossible to see how any human could stay on. At last came the pile driver, with the roan hunting the clouds and then coming down with all four legs stiff.

Brian shouted aloud in sympathetic reaction to the grinding shock. But Tiger had gone limp in the last moment and Snakebite might as well have tried to break a wet rag in two. The roan came out of the pile-driver windmilling insanely. But Tiger was still in leather.

They disappeared in the pall of dust again. The fence was lined with the horse runners who had come from other corrals to watch. Their excited shouting died as they stared at the cloud of dust, trying to tell from the sounds what was happening. The ground trembled to the pound of hoofs and a wild equine scream split the air. Then Tiger's roguish yell came out to them.

"Come on, you damn navvy, don't start crowhoppin' on me now, you ain't even showed me a sunfish yet —"

In another moment the horse came out of the dust again. He was no cyclone now. He was cat-backing and crow-hopping, pitching halfheartedly in a final gesture of defiance, a horse defeated yet still unwilling to give up. Tiger raked him with the spurs, trying to get another burst of violence from him. But the horse only squealed, cat-backed again, and then stopped completely.

He stood with four legs braced and head down, his ribs heaving like a bellows, the lather dripping from him dirty and yellow. The men gathered around, looking up at Tiger with the old awe in their faces, the old love. It wiped all the sophistication from Brian for that moment. It took him back to his childhood, when this man had been a towering god to him, a roaring, violent god, and Brian had never approached him without that awe, without that tremulous feeling of excitement and fear and worship all rolled into one.

Tiger had taken a terrific beating too. His cheeks were sunken and gray-looking, his eyes squinted as if in pain, and he was bleeding at the nose. But none of the men would give him the offense of offering help. The old man wiped blood from under his nose with the back of his hand, took a deep and shaken breath, and straightened up.

"Kaibab," he said, "next time will you accept my judgment on a horse?"

The bronc stomper shook his head, grimacing sheepishly at the ground. "I sure will, Mr. Sheridan, if you give me the chance."

"You got the chance," Tiger said. "Now git back to work — all you scalawags!"

The men scattered like a bunch of quail, leaving only Kaibab and the two hazers that had worked Snakebite. Stubs tucked his thumbs into sagging jeans.

"You want we should take him now, Mr. Sheridan?"

"Hell, no," Tiger said. "He's fit to work now and he needs some cooling down. I'll ride him out to roundup."

Brian started to protest again, then checked himself. He knew how useless it would be. Tiger's fierce old pride was working overtime. He had put on a show for his men and he was going to finish it.

"Wait for me to saddle up," Brian said. "I'll go with you."

Tiger turned an irascible scowl on him. He was still peeved with Brian for interfering with his treatment of Kaibab. "I don't need a nursemaid," he said. "Fetch me my hat, Stubs. Man can't go to work naked."

Stubs hobbled across the corral and picked up the battered hat. Brian took a last look at his father, then turned to walk down the line of corrals. In the last small pen nearest the house was a handful of the Sheridans' saddle horses. Brian's Steeldust was among them; he roped it out. As he was saddling up, Robles came from the kitchen door with an empty pail, heading toward the well. He saw Brian and changed his direction, coming over.

"He going to roundup?" Robles asked.

"I can't stop him," Brian said.

Robles glanced at the corrals. The adobe pen holding the unbroken horses blocked off the farther corrals and neither Tiger nor the horse handlers were visible. Without a word Robles put the pail down and went inside to rope out one of his pintos. They rode together back to the breaking corral. Tiger was not there, but Kaibab and Stubs were standing by the fence.

"Looked like he was takin' the Apache Trail," Stubs said.

"You better ketch up with him, Brian," Kaibab said. "One ride ain't going to bust that outlaw."

Brian and Robles put heels to their horses and left the ranch at a gallop. They followed a wagon road half a mile to the trail that had been cut through the matted growth by raiding Apaches who had followed the same course for a century.

47

That was history now and the trail had become a thoroughfare for cattlemen between the Rim and Apache Wells. Brian and the Indian pushed their horses for half an hour, but failed to come up with Tiger. Then they saw dust ahead and in a moment Latigo appeared on the trail.

He had always ridden a horse hard and his big Choppo was dripping lather and wheezing like a windsucker. He pulled it to a halt with a hard jerk on the reins and Brian went up to him.

"Did you pass Tiger?" Brian asked.

The foreman's jaw was blue with beard stubble and sweat lay like grease in the deep grooves about his mouth. "Didn't see him. I was coming in to find out about them fresh horses. Our remuda's down to the nub."

"You must have passed him," Brian said.

"I didn't see him, dammit."

Robles dropped off his pinto and crossed the trail, eyes squinted at the ground. Then he pointed at fresh tracks, unshod. "He come this way."

Latigo shoved back his greasy, flat-topped Stetson, scratching his black hair and scowling at Brian. Then he said, "We better have a look."

He wheeled the Choppo and all three of them headed down the trail, with Robles following sign all the way. In half a mile they came to a stretch where the hard ground had been cut up.

"Looks like his horse started pitching," Latigo said.

A pair of branches had been torn off on one

side of the trail and farther on more matted growth had been damaged. They followed the signs northward from the trail. It was like a swathe cut through the low, dense junipers. The horse had been pitching and fighting all the way, tearing a path through the undergrowth like a runaway locomotive. Then they came to a deep bank where an ancient, long-dry river had cut a channel through the rugged land thirty feet deep.

There was no sign of Snakebite. The horse had pitched his rider and run on. Tiger was doubled over, lying on his side at the bottom of the thirty foot drop. He looked like a man who had sat down to rest and fallen asleep.

4

They buried him the next day. They buried the king where he had always wanted to buried, up the Rim at the extreme western tip of his range, where the land dropped off sheer a thousand feet into the desert below and his dead eyes could look for an eternity on the vast expanse of the land he loved.

It was a long pull from Apache Wells. But they all came, the big and the little, the famous and the unknown, the banker and the storekeeper, the blacksmith and the stage clerk, the cattleman and the puncher — paying homage to the man they had revered. They packed densely around the grave while the minister read over the biggest of them all, and few of the men showed any shame for the tears in their eyes.

Robles stood apart. His face might have been carved from stone, so little sign did it give of the grief inside him. He had not spoken since they had found Tiger the day before.

The same grief was in Brian while he stood with George Wolffe and Arleen, listening to the minister.

And yet, moving turgidly beneath that grief, was the shadowy current of past resentments. He couldn't forget how bitterly they'd clashed the very day of Tiger's death. Like the taste of ashes in his mouth, it struck him that Tiger had never given him a chance while he lived — now he never could.

Now, he supposed, all the others would be expecting him to step right up and fill the old man's boots. But how could he, the way Tiger had insisted on ruling the roost his own way? Ah, the hell with it . . .

Brian shook the thoughts off. That was a sleazy way to be thinking now. He *had* loved the old man, in his way, he tried to assure himself. He wished he could have gotten together with Tiger before his death. Well, it was too late now.

After the simple ceremony was finished the people crowded around Brian with their condolences. He went through the motions in a numb misery, talking, nodding, shaking hands. Finally Arleen extricated him and took him to the buckboard. George Wolffe followed. He was in his cheap black town suit, his square and massive face pale and drawn above the stiff white collar.

"We'll drive you home," he said.

"Maybe he'd rather be alone," Arleen said softly.

"Nonsense," Wolffe said. "What good are friends if they can't try to help somehow at a time like this? Best thing is to take your mind off it, Brian. You'll never do it alone."

51

Brian stared at the ground. "Maybe you're right," he said at last. While Wolffe went to get his horse Brian listlessy helped Arleen into the rig and followed her up. He wished he were a woman. He wished he could cry like a woman. There must be some way to give vent to the pain in him. He slumped over in the seat, gazing blankly ahead, the lines drawn deep about his mouth. Arleen's hand crept into his.

Latigo threaded his way through the crowd, riding his Choppo horse. His hat was in his hand and for once the insolence did not show in his eyes. He stopped by the buckboard, moistened his lips.

"This is a bad time to ask, Brian. But I better know about the round up."

Brian continued looking blankly ahead. A strange lethargy seemed to have settled over him, an apathy, an overwhelming sense of the futility of words. Arleen squeezed his hand.

"Brian."

"What?" He straightened, glanced at her, then at Latigo. He passed a hand over his eyes and shook his head. "I'm sorry." What had Latigo said? "The roundup." He squinted his eyes shut, trying to think clearly. "I know what a blow this is to the whole crew, Latigo. Try to keep it going. Tell them it's what Tiger would want. I'll be down to see about things as soon as possible."

Latigo lifted his reins and pulled the Choppo horse around and walked it away. Wolffe had hitched Brian's Steeldust to the tail-gate and he climbed aboard and picked up the reins. They rattled across the stone flat onto the trail. The desert looked like another world, so far below, running out to mesas that cut the horizon into a broken mauve pattern, fifty miles away. A strange hush hung over the Rim, as it had that evening they found Nacho with the Double Bit cattle.

It made Brian turn to look at Robles. The old Indian had not wanted Tiger to follow those cattle. He had asked Brian to stop Tiger from going out to roundup the day he had died.

"George," Brian said, "do you really think those Indians know things we don't?"

"Haven't you seen enough of it to know?" Wolffe said. He glanced aside at Brian. "Why?"

"Nothing."

Brian looked again at Robles, standing alone now by the grave. The old Indian's head was raised and he was staring off at the majestic cloud masses forming above the ghostly ramparts of the Superstitions far to the south.

The ride back to the Double Bit was interminable. Only Wolffe tried to make conversation, but Brian was in no mood to sustain it. Finally Wolffe gave up and drove in sober silence, while a rising wind carried the parched scent of early fall from the desert below. The other wagon appeared behind them, carrying Juanita, the Mexican housekeeper, and Pinto, the old cow-camp cook Tiger had taken into the household when a stampede had crippled him fifteen years before. They reached the house by sundown and Wolffe offered to stay with Brian if it would do any good. Thinking of those forty empty rooms and of the terrible loneliness he had known the night before, Brian welcomed the offer and invited them to dinner.

Juanita served them, dabbing constantly at tears that welled into her eyes. None of them had any appetite, and they left most of the food on the table. Afterward Brian built a fire in the living-room and they tried to talk, but it was no good. Finally he told them he was going to bed and excused himself.

He couldn't sleep. He didn't even undress. He sat in his big rawhide-seated chair and smoked and paced the floor for hours. He remembered his father pacing the same way, fifteen years ago, when his mother had died. He had been too young then for the full depth of the old man's grief to reach him. He understood it better now. He understood the look Tiger had given the door of her room whenever he passed it in the hall. Why did such understanding have to wait till now? Why couldn't he have known the old man better ten years ago? A month ago? He ground an unsmoked cigarette under his heel and sat down on the bed.

The Wolffes stayed for several days, but George had his own business to take care of and finally they had to leave, making Brian promise he would come in to see them soon.

In all that time, Robles had not returned. Brian knew that the old Indian was probably back on the reservation somewhere, alone with the earth and the sky, communicating his grief to his own ancient gods.

Brian woke early the morning after the Wolffes left, and dressed and went to breakfast. Walking down the hall, he saw that the door to Tiger's room was open. Just inside, gazing blankly at the empty brass bed, was Robles. The greasy dust-chalked *chivarras* sheathing his skinny legs emanated the pungent scent of sage and pine and tallow. Over a cotton shirt he wore a blue velvet vest, faded and tawdry, and the huge silver bosses on his belt gave off a tarnished shimmer. Grief and fasting had made almost a skull of his gaunt old head; the hollows were sunk deep beneath his cheekbones and the muscles in his neck stood against the sallow skin like pale strings. Brian felt awkward before him, inarticulate. Yet he wanted to talk with Robles.

He walked restlessly past the Indian, staring at the bed. He was remembering how he had laughed at the Apache's forebodings and superstitions through the last months. Was this what Robles had feared? Could he have had the prescience to foresee Tiger's death?

"You didn't want him to go out to roundup that day, did you?" he murmured. Robles did not answer, and Brian continued. "You spoke of signs, Robles. What signs? Did they tell of this?"

Robles was silent so long Brian thought he

would not speak. Finally his voice came, dry and rustling as the whisper of dying leaves in the wind. "Bad sign. In the sky. On the earth —"

His voice trailed off. Brian knew he would get no more out of the man. He had been as vague before, unable or unwilling to communicate the nebulous prophesies conjured out of his primitive attunement to the earth and the sky. Brian circled the room, feeling the gap between them, the weight of the patriarch's disapproval. But it held none of Latigo's scorn; it was more a thing of pity, of doubt. Despite the man's censure, Brian admired Robles, and had always wanted his respect.

"Pinto says you'll return to your people," Brian said. A flicker touched Robles' filmed, sunken eyes, but he did not answer. Brian fought with his pride and then looked squarely at Robles. "I want you to stay. I'll need your help." Again Robles did not answer. But his attention swung briefly to the bed, and Brian understood the implications. "I know you think I can't ever fill his boots, Robles. Maybe nobody could. Do I have to be as big as Tiger to be a man? I'll try to measure up. I'll have to, if I mean to hold the Double Bit together."

Robles turned and stared unwinkingly at him, it was like having his soul stripped bare. Finally his dry lips moved.

"I will stay."

Brian felt a surge of triumph. This was more acceptance than he had ever gotten from Robles before. But he knew he was merely on probation. If he failed to measure up, the last feeble bond between them would be severed.

"Can you eat now?" he asked. Robles nodded. "Let's have breakfast," Brian said. "Afterward we can go out to roundup. It'll help us keep our minds off him."

The roundup grounds were on the high, rolling land north of the Double Bit. Between two low ridges lay a mile-long, juniper-covered flat. At its lower end was a pole corral for the remuda, jam-packed with fresh mounts; beyond it were two dozen saddled animals picketed to a rope line, waiting to replace used-up cutters and ropers. Three wranglers, no more than tow-headed kids, squatted on their heels against the pole fence, smoking and talking horses. A hundred yards on, camp began, a welter of spare saddles, warbags, blankets, and heaped gear. At its farther edge stood the wagons — freight, chuck, and calf — tongues dropped and tailgates down. A pair of swampers were heaving hundred-pound sacks of flour from the bed of the freight outfit. The roustabout was raising a hellish clatter as he cleaned breakfast dishes and the cook was busy butchering a calf for son-of-a-gun stew.

The inevitable curtain of dust hung over the farther flats; half visible in this buttery haze was the saffron flicker of branding fires, the shadowy forms of riders passing back and forth, the countless white faces of the cattle like flakes of snow tossing on the black sea of their bodies.

Brian found Latigo at one of the fires, dust-caked, sweating, riding his men with a constant volley of orders. He turned in the saddle as Brian approached.

"I'm going to finish roundup with you," Brian said.

Latigo's eyes swung to Robles. The Indian said nothing. Latigo looked at Brian again. A sardonic grin touched his mouth.

"Tiger wanted to teach you the business a long time ago."

"I know it. I guess I wasn't ready then. I am now."

For a moment Latigo seemed to be taking a new measure of Brian. Then he tilted his head to one side. "I'll show you the cutting."

At the cutting grounds two thousand cattle were being held by the crooning circle riders. New bunches were constantly being added by the combers as they came in from remote sections of the range. One pair of cutters was working the late calves that had been missed that spring, freeing them from the main herd with their mothers and driving them to the fire. Here the branding teams threw the calves, burned the Double Bit into their hides, and earmarked them.

"They'll go into the cutbacks over in that coulee," Latigo said. "When roundup's over we'll turn 'em back to open range. The beef cut is what you'll be interested in."

Another man was cutting a big bay steer free of the same main herd and driving him in the other direction from the branding fires. Latigo and Brian followed through a pall of dust to the roundup pens, sprawled out for half a mile across the north end of the flat. These pens were filled with the steers destined for market. Brian knew enough about beef on the hoof to see what good condition they were in.

"Fat'n sassy," he said.

"Tiger made us work 'em slow," Latigo told him. "He said every drop of sweat was a pound of beef lost."

A rider on a lathered black came through the fog of dust toward them. Brian saw it was Wirt Peters. He was big in the saddle, heat giving his flesh a ruddy glow through the scrubby blond beard. His blue shirt was plastered to his beefy muscles with sweat, and brush-scars made illegible etchings in the film of dust graying his batwing chaps. A mottled bruise still remained on his face from the fight with Tiger at the Black Jack. He reined up before them, nodding a greeting.

"I been trailing a big drift of my three-year-olds up from the Rim," he said. "Figure your combers gathered them in about ten miles south."

"We didn't spot none of your earmarks," Latigo said.

"I'd like a look."

"You calling me a liar?"

"Hell, no. Isn't it possible you overlooked 'em?"

The cutter had pushed his beef into the pen and was sitting his horse by the pole fence, watching intently. Two other punchers handling the gate stood near by, their attention on the scene. Latigo put raw-knuckled hands on the saddle horn and settled forward, his face bleak.

"If they're in our herd, we'd of seen 'em, Peters. Now you better turn around and go home."

"Hold it," Brian said. He couldn't understand Latigo's anger. "As long as he's here you might as well let him have a look."

Latigo's slope-shouldered body stiffened and his head turned sharply to Brian. The shimmering ridge of his cheeks stood out white as bone against the angry red of his face. Before he could speak a puncher came in at a lope, calling to the ramrod.

"Daggett just came in with some stuff that looks blotted. You better have a look."

Latigo frowned, hesitated, then swung his sullen gaze back to Peters. "If you're not out of here when I get back I'm goin' to tie a can to your tail."

He raked a glance across Brian, then spurred his horse viciously after the puncher.

"What's the matter with him?" Brian asked.

Peters grinned ruefully. "Reckon he's still mad about how I clobbered him at the Black Jack."

He continued to look questioningly at Brian. The cutter and the two punchers by the gate were still watching, and Brian realized he had put himself in a bad spot. He had already questioned Latigo's decision; if he backed down now it would be taken as a sign of weakness. What would Tiger do? He remembered the incident with Snakebite.

"How about it, Brian?" Peters asked.

Brian tried not to look at the watching punchers. Peters had come half a day's ride after those strays. It would be ridiculous to turn him back without a look.

"Go ahead," he said.

The beefy man grinned and touched his hat, then turned his black into the haze of dust. The cutter glanced closely at the two punchers by the gate and something seemed to pass between them. Then the man spurred his horse back to the main herd. Brian followed, watching Peters circle the herd. Under the circumstances it was almost impossible to read the brands of any cattle save those on the outer fringes, and it was the earmarks a man looked for. Brian could see nothing but the Double Bit's famous swallow-fork on any of the ears. Finally Peters left the main herd and dropped into the coulee where the cutbacks were held. This smaller bunch of newly branded calves and their mothers was being guarded by a single circle rider — a tall, snuff-brown man named Hollister.

Brian checked his horse idly at the lip of the

coulee, watching Peters skirt the fringes again. Then the man turned his horse abruptly into the cattle, shouldering through the bawling mass of beef until he came to a big dun cow. He put his horse against her and started to cut her out of the main bunch. Hollister came in after Peters, yelling at him. Brian was too far away to hear what was said, or to see clearly what happened.

Latigo came back from his chore, trotting out of the dust and checking his horse beside Brian with a vicious tug on the reins. "What's Peters doing down there?" he asked.

"I let him go," Brian said. "There wasn't any point in sending him back without a look."

Latigo's gaunt head swung toward him. For a moment Brian thought the man would explode. Then Latigo settled back into the saddle, hands white-knuckled on his reins. His lips were pale, barely moving as he spoke.

"Five years ago Tiger made a deal with the Salt River bunch that they weren't to send any straymen north of the river."

"You didn't tell me," Brian said.

"I thought you knew *something*," Latigo told him disgustedly. "The Salt River Gorge forms a natural barrier. In five years our combers have only picked up three of Peters's steers. There's no need for him to come up here."

"But he said he followed strays."

Latigo shook his head angrily. "With Tiger gone, they're just seein' how far they can push you. He'll claim every maverick in our herds,

62

and not a one of 'em his. Damn it, Brian!"

He wheeled his horse and started to put it down into the coulee. Peters and the circle rider were still arguing in the middle of the herd. Hollister was trying to keep Peters from cutting the cow out but the Salt River man would not be stopped. As he tried to maneuver the animal past Hollister, the man yanked his Winchester from his boot and put it across the saddle bows.

Peters glared at the gun a long time. Hollister jerked his head for the man to move and Peters started out of the herd. As he passed Hollister a shift in the herd jostled into them. Hollister tried to catch himself and it swung his Winchester aside. Peters made a grab for the gun. Hollister tried to swing it back, finger on the trigger, and the jar of hitting Peters's hand made it go off.

The detonation made a shocking sound. It sent a surge of panic through the cutbacks, like ripples spreading from a rock dropped into a pool. Those nearest the men began bucking and kicking and lunging to get away. It ran through the outer ranks in a chain reaction and those on the fringes began to bolt down the coulee.

On the flank of the herd, Latigo put spurs to his horse and raced to turn the beef already running. He signaled to Brian. "Git down here and make a mill. If they stampede they'll go right into the main herd."

His strident voice was barely audible over the growing thunder of running animals. Hollister and Peters were fighting over the gun in the middle of it all and their struggles only increased the panic. The whole herd was right on the edge of stampede and they would be gone in another moment.

Brian put his Steeldust down the sandy bank on its rump and raced after Latigo, driving the bunch quitters back as they broke from the mass of the herd and tried to climb the bank. The two men in the center were being buffeted back and forth by the panicked animals all about them and had finally realized their peril.

Wirt Peters released the Winchester and drove his horse through the bawling cows toward the outside. Latigo had reached the running steers near the mouth of the coulee now and was trying to turn them back. But the body of the herd was moving into a run after him. Once they left the coulee nothing but a few hundred yards of open flats stood between them and the main herd. Three hundred cutbacks charging head-on into the thousands of cattle spread out across the flats would start a stampede the whole Double Bit crew couldn't stop.

Brian's racing horse took him up behind Latigo and the ramrod shouted at him and waved directions with his arm. "Turn 'em left. Get 'em milling, it's our only chance." Latigo saw Wirt Peters breaking free from the running bunch and shouted at him. "Up here, damn you. Mill 'em. Up here."

Latigo had his hat off, popping it against his leg. The frightening sound made the lead steers shy away from him, veering left. Peters joined them, yelling and popping his hat too. The pressure of all three horsemen got the head of the running herd turned back on itself. Some of them plunged headlong into the sandy bank and went down, trampled by those behind; others managed to get turned around, evading the shouting, shoving riders, and began to run back the way they had come. The main body of the herd, forced by the riders, blindly followed their leaders, and the mill was started.

It was then that Brian saw Hollister again. The man had managed to get near the outer fringe of running steers. But the leaders turning back had charged right into him. His horse fought for a moment but the constant buffeting of animals from both directions took it off balance.

In a single instant the horse went down and Hollister sank beneath the sea of dark, plunging bodies like a drowning man.

Without thought, Brian wheeled his Steeldust and drove it into the mass of cattle toward the spot where the man had gone down. Wirt Peters was but a hundred feet behind him, fighting to keep the beef in the mill, and the man shouted frantically at him, "Brian, don't do it, they'll suck you under like a bog!"

But Brian was already in the vortex. The cows were still running insanely, trying to break free of the mill on the outside and climb the bank. Their frenzied bawling deafened Brian and the sand boiled up in choking clouds. He couldn't help shouting in pain as their sweating bodies slammed with numbing impact against his legs.

He could feel the Steeldust dancing beneath him, trying to keep its feet as thousands of pounds of beef buffeted into it from every side. Ahead of him Brian saw a calf stumble and go down, trampled in an instant.

A half-wild cow hooked at Brian and he had to jerk aside to keep from being impaled. Another cow crashed against him on the other side, almost dragging him from the saddle. The Steeldust was wild with panic, squealing and frothing at the mouth, fighting the bit like a green bronc.

Finally Brian caught a glimpse of Hollister ahead. The man's horse had fallen on him and it was the only thing that had saved him. The cows were eddying around the body of the horse and as yet hadn't trampled him. Brian fought his Steeldust in close, shouting down at the man.

"Hollister, can you hear me? Hollister!"

The man opened fogged eyes, turning his head up. His feeble call was barely audible above the other bedlam. "I can't make it. I'm pinned under. My legs is broke for sure."

Brian sidled his horse right above the man, kicking a stirrup out. "Grab hold. We'll haul you out."

Hollister made a lunge for the stirrup and caught hold, hooking an arm through clear to the elbow. Brian spurred the horse and it lunged aside. Hollister let out a scream of agony as his broken legs were pulled free.

Brian bent over, meaning to pull the man up. A big dun cow crashed against him, pinning him to the horse. For a moment he thought he would be dragged from the saddle. Then the cow shifted away and he regained his seat with a desperate lunge.

"Don't try it again or we'll both be pulled down," Hollister gasped. "Just let the horse git us out."

Brian knew that was the only way now. The Steeldust was a cowpony, born and bred. Frantic as it was, it could not forget its training. As long as Brian was in the saddle to guide it, they had a chance. Like a top cutter the horse fought its way through the milling mass of steers, wheeling into openings, making holes if there were none, shouldering aside steers and veering away from traps, dragging Hollister all the way.

A spotted calf trampled Hollister's feet, bringing another yell of pain. Brian leaned out of the saddle, screaming at a following cow. It veered around Hollister, just missing his legs. Finally they were at the fringe of the herd. Brian put spurs to the Steeldust and it lunged up the crumbling, sandy bank of the coulee, pulling the crippled man along.

At the top Hollister let his arm slide from the stirrup and lay flat on the ground. His face was buried in the dirt and his fingers were clawed into the ground with the pain of his legs. Circle riders had come from the main herd and the branding fires now, to hold the cutbacks in their mill.

With the danger of stampede over, Latigo drove his lathered Choppo horse up the bank to where Brian knelt beside Hollister.

"Get a wagon up here," Brian said. "He's hurt pretty bad."

Latigo relayed the order in a bawling voice and one of the circle riders galloped off toward camp. Latigo got off his horse. His clothes were ripped in a dozen places and one leg was smeared with blood. Dust caked him head to foot, turned to a paste by the sweat on his face. His heavylidded eyes were bloodshot with a seething rage as he looked at Hollister, then back at Wirt Peters, pushing his winded horse up the bank.

The beefy Salt River man swung down. He took off his hat, crumpling the brim in his hand, and wiped the sweat and grime from his face with a sleeve. "I didn't mean anything like that," he said. "I was sure that cow belonged to me —"

"So you start a stampede," Latigo said. His voice was trembling. His whole lanky body was trembling.

"I didn't mean anything like that," Peters said. He motioned helplessly at Hollister with his hat. "Isn't there something I can do?"

"Jist get out of here," said Latigo.

The man moistened his lips. "Now, wait —"

"Peters!" Latigo said.

The venom in his voice stopped Peters. Slowly the big man turned and swung aboard his horse. The calf wagon came rattling across the coulee, hauled by a pair of half-broke broncs, and plunged up the bank to halt beside Hollister. A pair of punchers dropped out and helped Brian and Latigo lift the crippled man into the blankets spread on the bed.

"Split up some cottonwood for slats and tie 'em on them legs," Latigo told the men. "Then take him right into town."

Latigo watched the wagon pull away. Then he turned to Brian. He was no longer trembling but the rage was in his eyes.

"I know it's too late to apologize," Brian said. "But I had no idea —"

"Didn't you think I had a good reason for not letting Peters in?" Latigo said. "Every time those Salt Rivers sent a strayman in we had trouble. This is just one example. It's why Tiger made the deal with 'em. I can't have you crossing me up all the time like this. Tiger thought I was good enough to run my own show. It you don't, I'll be glad to check out. But it's got to be one way or the other. Either I'm boss out here or I'm not. If I'm not, the rodeo is all yours."

Brian felt anger and pride stiffening him like a ramrod. But he knew he'd be a fool to let it sway him. He had to admit Latigo was right, and he knew how good Latigo was at his job. He would be a fool to lose such a man. It hurt like hell to swallow his pride, to humble himself before this man. But if he was ever going to grow up, this was a chance to start.

"All right, Latigo," he said. "It's your job."

5

After that Brian had to choose between the defeat of leaving roundup or the misery of staying. He knew what he would face, in the men, by remaining. Yet the stubbornness in him and the pride made him stick.

Every minute was painful. He had no part in the work, the men found little cause to speak with him, and Latigo made no attempt to help him. For the most part Brian stayed moodily around camp, drinking coffee and smoking, or sat his horse with Robles, watching the cutting and roping and branding.

The evening meal was worse. The men were as embarrassed as he was. By his mistake that afternoon he had wiped out whatever ground he had to meet them on. His presence at the camp fire made for a stiff and gloomy meal. What the punchers thought of him was apparent. They held him responsible for Hollister being crippled, for the whole mess that afternoon. And the fact that he had risked his life to save Hollister wasn't enough. Brian had known most of these men, casually, all his life. Yet he felt like a stranger at their campfire.

He slept little that night and was the first man up at dawn. After breakfast the men left hurriedly, as if relieved to be out of his presence. Again he was relegated to the role of observer. Having agreed not to interfere with Latigo's authority, he could give no orders, and there seemed no natural reason for contact with the men. He thought desperately of getting in and working with them. But he knew little of roping or cutting, would only make a further fool of himself, and any such thing would be a pathetically obvious attempt to curry favor with them.

The whole operation was obviously being handled so efficiently that Brian had no valid reason for staying on. Thus, during the second day, unable to face the ostracism, frustrated by a defeat he could hardly define, Brian returned to the Double Bit with Robles.

The Indian left him at the corrals and miserably Brian walked in and fixed himself a drink. After an hour Pinto hobbled in from the kitchen to tell him dinner was ready. The old cook rubbed his twisted leg.

"Winter in the air when she begins to ache like this." He grimaced. "Robles told me 'bout Hollister's legs. Hope he don't end up like me."

Brian scowled into his drink. "I was a fool, Pinto."

"We all make mistakes," Pinto said. "You had to learn the hard way. Latigo's a good man,

Brian. A smart boss gets a good man, he don't interfere much."

"Then what's there for me to do?" Brian said. "I wanted to be a part of it, Pinto, to get my teeth in something."

"It'll take time, Brian. You can't just go out and take over in a day. What Tiger had with 'em went back a long way."

"Maybe you're right," Brian said.

"Why don't you go in and see George Wolffe? He wanted you to go over the books. That's somethin' you can git your teeth in."

Brian nodded. George had pounded him for years to learn the business end of running the ranch. Perhaps he would meet with more success there.

The next morning he rode into Apache Wells early. As he dropped down off the Rim he could see the heliograph twinkle from the windows of the town ten miles off. It made him think of Tiger and remember how they had always bet on which one would see it first.

There was not much traffic on Cochise Street. He passed a wagon going out, piled high with hay. Standing before the curlicued façade of the Mercantile was a shabby spring buggy. Pa Gillette had just climbed down. He was one of the dry farmers from south of the Salt, a gaunt and gnarled man whose face was seamed and furrowed like a haphazardly plowed field. He wore blue jeans held up by a single gallus, so ingrained with filth they looked black. In the buggy was his daughter, Estelle. She was a richly formed girl in simple blue calico, her hazel eyes flecked with little lights as tawny as her honey-colored hair. There was something intensely wholesome about the whole picture — always making Brian think of summer corn and fresh-baked bread and the cleansing scent of a spring wind. Brian never failed to make his bid whenever he saw her, but she was seldom in town, and it was his rueful complaint that she was one of the few girls who had failed to succumb to his charms.

He checked his horse beside the buggy and removed his hat, greeting them both. Then he spoke directly to Estelle. "Been longer than usual this time. You turning into a hermit?"

Her full lips formed a reserved smile. It was this composure that had always checked the flippancy with which he treated most women. "A lot of work on the farm this year," she said.

His blue eyes twinkled. "All work and no play —"

Her smile did not grow. "Better dull than lazy."

He bowed his head in defeat. "A victory for the righteous."

Pa Gillette was not particularly pleased with the exchange. He had always been one of those who did not bother to hide their disapproval of Brian. But now he seemed to have something on his mind. He took off his hat and scratched gnarled fingers through his gray hair, roached short like a mule's mane. Then he looked at Brian.

"I been meaning to come out your way. I wanted to know if Tiger's promise still held good."

"What promise, Mr. Gillette?"

"About six months ago I got me forty acres of bottomland from the bank. It was a deal I'd been tryin' to swing for years and the only way I could do it was on a short-term loan. Tiger holds a regular mortage on my other land but he said I could let the payments lapse till I paid off this new forty. Now Wolffe wants to go back on the promise."

"If you had Tiger's word you have mine," Brian said. He expected it to dissolve some of the patent hostility in Pa Gillette's face. But the man only scowled deeply and asked, "How can I be sure?"

"What more do you want?"

The man spat disgustedly. "I dunno. How good's your word? You beat the hell out of Cameron in that saloon brawl. You won't let Wirt Peters look for his own strays."

"You know the agreement Tiger made with the Salt Rivers," Brian said angrily. "Wirt didn't have any right up there. He's as much to blame for Hollister getting mangled as anybody."

"If Hollister got hurt it's his own fault."

Brian bent toward the man, trying to hold on to his temper. "You can't be that blind, Pa."

A sullen flush crept into the man's face; he

stepped to Brian's horse and clutched the head-stall with a knobby hand. His eyes were piggish with an old man's irascible anger.

"When our bunch made that agreement not to send any straymen north of the Salt," he said, "it was reasonable. Not many of our cattle drifted up on the Rim and what did was all sent back. But these last two or three years we been losing more and more stock on the drift. And they don't come back."

The inference brought a rush of hot blood to Brian's face. Estelle saw it and tried to placate him. "We know the men on the Rim are too big to operate that way, Brian. They wouldn't gain anything by hanging on to what little stuff drifts up from the desert."

Brian glanced at her, unable to keep a sharpness from his voice. "Then why bring it up?"

"I don't know." She sent a troubled glance at Pa, continuing swiftly as though to keep him from offending Brian again. "We talked to Tiger a while back. He blamed our missing beef on those penny-ante border hoppers that're always coming over. But that doesn't answer it. There's something strange going on all over the range."

The phrase took away some of Brian's anger. "Funny you should put it that way. Robles said the same thing." He couldn't help turning to look off at the vague shape of the Superstitions, lying northwest of town. "He's been talking about strange signs for a long time. He couldn't put his finger on anything, but he knew something was happening."

She was looking in the same direction, and she asked, in a hushed voice, "Do you suppose it comes from these renegades in the Superstitions?"

"Renegades, hell," Pa said. "We know where it comes from."

Brian's eyes flashed and his sharp jerk on the reins made the horse toss its head, jerking the headstall from Pa's loose grip.

"Pa, don't be a fool," Estelle said heatedly. "You ask his help and then you insult him." She turned to Brian. "Forget what he said. We're in trouble, Brian, and everybody's jumpy. We do want to work it out with you." She hesitated, eyes dark. Then she asked, "You'll keep Tiger's promise, won't you?"

He held his fiddling horse for a moment, looking into her soft face, her pleading eyes. A wind whirled alkali against the Steeldust and it stamped and fretted.

"For you, I'll keep it," he said. He glanced at Pa, tight-lipped with disgust, and wheeled the horse around to gallop down the street. A block from them he turned off onto a meandering side street to see Hollister, who was at his brother's house, a block from the Black Jack. The man was resting easy, both legs in splints, and the doctor said the wound would heal all right. He tried to be cheerful but Brian could see the man was uncomfortable in his presence. He left in a little while, promising Hollister full pay while he was convalescing. After that he went to Wolffe's office.

He found the lawyer bent over a pile of papers on his desk, studying them in the dim light from dusty windows. Wolffe pushed them aside and rose, extending a hand to Brian. His smile was quick, and a little strained.

"Glad you came, Brian. I hear you've really settled down. Working on the roundup and everything."

Brian tossed his hat onto a chair, ran a hand through unruly red hair. "Afraid I didn't do so good there, George."

"Don't be discouraged."

"I ran into the Gillettes this morning. Pa said Tiger had promised him a breather on his note till he got that new land paid off."

Wolffe's lips compressed. He locked his hands behind his back and paced angrily to a window. "He came to me too. How do we know Tiger gave any such promise?"

"We can't go back on Tiger's word."

"But Gillette has no proof of any such agreement. If we honor this, a hundred men will be in here with all kinds of fantastic claims about Tiger's promises."

"Is this part of the business I was supposed to learn?"

Wolffe returned to the desk. "At least it will teach you what *not* to do." He slid open a drawer and pulled out a handful of bank books and three ledgers with the Double Bit burned into their leather covers. "Here's something a little more tangible than supposed verbal agreements. It's long past time you studied them."

Brian pulled a chair to the desk and they both sat down. Wolffe went through the bank books with him, the drawing account, the ranch account, the business account. It was all fairly simple and didn't take too long. Then came the ledgers. They covered all the business of the vast Double Bit enterprise, the cattle sales and purchases, the operation of Tiger's mercantile establishments in Apache Wells and Tucson, the countless land transactions that Tiger had been involved with. It was surprising how many notes and mortgages Tiger had bought up around Apache Wells in the last years. Half the men in the county seemed to owe him money.

Wolffe insisted on going over each item in great detail. Gradually, as he patiently explained the complexities of the figures, the picture began to emerge for Brian, and he felt a return of his old frustration. George Wolffe was handling this end of the operation as efficiently as Latigo was handling his.

"As far as I can make out you've got the Double Bit going along just great," Brian said.

"Don't be too optimistic."

Brian shook his head. "That's what I like about you, George. All the investments you've made are paying off handsomely. Only a couple of men behind in their notes. Latigo's shipping beef that averages out ten pounds heavier than any other rancher in the valley. Cattle prices are up. And you say don't be optimistic."

George rose and walked to the window. "Your problem isn't all financial. Tiger was a key man in the politics of this town. With him gone, the Salt River bunch is going to try and get in the saddle. This affair with the Gillettes is an example. They'll be on you from every side."

Brian remembered the incident with Wirt Peters at roundup and again knew an uneasy prescience of trouble. Yet what trouble? Brian had known vaguely that there was a clash between the shoestring ranchers south of the Salt and the few big operators up in the Rim country. But he'd never paid much attention to politics and in the last years had seen little evidence of conflict. As a matter of fact, Tiger had kept many of the smaller Salt River operators in business during the lean years.

"Let's finish with the books first," Brian said. "What happens if I learn all about them?" He saw a blankness come to Wolffe's face and he added, "That's what I mean, George. How often did Tiger go over the books with you?"

"Not often enough."

"Every six months?"

"If that often."

Brian shoved back his chair, the picture complete now. "That's a big job," he said. "Won't leave me much time on the outside."

"Brian, you've got to take this seriously."

"Sure, George." Brian rose and picked up his

hat. He walked moodily to the door. "How about a drink?"

"Don't start that. We haven't finished."

"Later, George. Got to get back to roundup. They can't get by very long without me, you know."

Alkali sifted out of the hot street like cornstarch. The late afternoon sun turned westward windows to blazing copper. Brian walked down the rickety stairs from Wolffe's office, bitter and moody.

What had they all wanted him to do when they had pounded him to settle down? The whole thing was running by itself. Latigo could obviously handle the cattle operation without ever seeing a boss. And he had felt like a fifth wheel in Wolffe's office, an observer again, watching a man conduct business ten times as efficiently as Brian himself could. Sometimes Wolffe seemed almost too efficient, as though he were owner of the Double Bit and every cent Brian spent was somehow money out of his own pocket. Then Brian realized he was probably just trying to justify himself. Wolffe was just doing his job — and damn well, too.

An intense restlessness swept Brian. The frustration was like a pressure building up in him, seeking some release. He saw Charlie Casket standing at the door of the Black Jack, cadavarous as an undertaker in his black clawhammer coat. His lusterless eyes were sunk deep in a sallow face and his black hair was shiny as varnish and plastered against his bony skull. He held out a pack of cards and his voice ran across the street like a sardonic whisper.

"Pick a card, Brian."

Welcoming the diversion. Brian walked across the street, taking one of the cards. He looked at it without letting Casket see. It was an ace of spades. He slid the card back into the deck, face down, and then took the deck from Casket's hand. He shuffled it twice and then fanned it and held it out to Casket. The man chose a card and turned its face up. It was an ace of spades.

The old trick brought some of Brian's humor back. He grinned at Casket. "When you going to miss, Charlie?"

The man never smiled. "Haven't seen you around, Brian. You aren't turning parson on us?"

Jess Miller appeared in the door of his Mercantile, saw Brian, and came down the walk to the saloon. He was the picture of plump prosperity in his rust-colored fustian and tailored broadcloth pants. A friendly grin wreathed his round face and he clapped Brian on the shoulder.

"Good to see you in circulation again, Brian. Going to join us?"

"I guess that's just about what I need," Brian said.

They went into the gloomy adobe room smelling of damp sawdust and cheap whisky and the homemade grape wine the Mexicans loved so much. A scattering of men stood at the bar. Near the rear Brian saw Nacho and Ford Tarrant playing black jack. Tarrant was one of the big operators on the Rim, a squarely framed, hearty man in his mid-forties. He hailed them, asking them to sit in. Brian took a chair beside Nacho and Jigger brought over a fresh bottle.

They drank and Brian put his glass down empty. "Ford, how do you manage to spend so much time in town? I bet they never see you at home."

Tarrant laughed jovially. "The secret is to have a good manager, like you, Brian. I'll give you ten thousand dollars for Latigo and twice as much for Wolffe."

Casket had begun to deal and Brian picked up his hand, fanning the cards. "Not for sale, Ford. I guess I didn't know how valuable they were till today."

They emptied the bottle before the hand was up. Brian knew he was drinking too much. The stakes were high and he was losing and sometime in the early afternoon he sent one of Jigger's housemen to the bank with a note for more money.

Later a girl called Nita floated in. She was one of a score he had romanced, a girl from West Cochise, the section of adobe *jacales* and tar-paper huts removed from the more respectable section of town by Indian Creek. A round little face, deceptively wide eyes, a mouth too full. A woman who could love you one minute and knife you the next.

She watched the game for a while. Full-blown breasts pressed against Brian's shoulder as she kibitzed, running slender fingers through his hair.

"Nita, howthehell can a man play cards?"

"Who wants to play cards, *mi corazón?*"

He looked at her big black eyes, her shimmering lips. She was right. The cards weren't doing him any good. He couldn't seem to drink enough. How did a man forget?

Nita smiled. "Why don't we go somewhere, *mi corazón?*"

At seven in the morning most of Apache Wells was still asleep. The sun was up but light came off the desert like reflection from a window, glowing, luminous, a little unworldly. Brian's boots kicked up hollow echoes as he crossed the sagging plank bridge over Indian Creek. His mouth felt like a hundred pinto ponies had tramped through it in their stocking feet. His head ached unmercifully and the light made his eyes water when he kept them open. Squinting and stumbling, he made his way down Cochise.

It hadn't helped much. He wouldn't mind paying for it like this if it had helped. But none of it had helped. The cards. The drinking. Nita. Why had he thought she could help?

He felt like hell.

He figured somebody had put his horse in the stables so he headed that way. He was passing the feed store when he saw Arleen step out of Jess Miller's place across the way, a sack of coffee in her hands. He had no impulse to avoid the meeting. She had seen him like this too often before. She crossed to him, pursing her lips as she looked at his puffy eyes. Her voice was matter-of-fact.

"You could clean up a little."

"Don't want to wake George."

"He left early for Alta. Some case."

He looked at the coffee, grinning faintly. "Some of that would help."

Without a word she led him upstairs. While she put the coffee on he went into George's room and shaved. He was halfway through when she came to the door. She regarded him soberly for a moment, hands clasped in front of her. Finally she said:

"Help any?"

He groaned.

"You needed something," she said. "Tiger's death was a terrible blow."

"More than that, Arleen. The books, the roundup. They want me to settle down but they won't let me. There's nothing for me to do."

"You found plenty to do before," she said. Her voice had a strange, stiff sound. "Why try to change? They haven't got any right to tell you what to do."

He looked up, surprised by the outburst.

A little muscle twitched in her throat. "I guess I've kept quiet too long. All of them preaching at you and pounding at you. So you didn't make out on roundup. You never cared what the crew thought of you before. They live in a different world, Brian. They'd look just as silly trying to live in yours. You had a good life. You were happy, everybody was your friend. Why try to twist things out of shape?" She made an impatient sound, and shook her head sharply. "I sound like George now — preaching."

She went back into the kitchen. He stared at the empty door, puzzled. But his head hurt too much to think. He finished shaving and washed up and then went into the kitchen in his shirt sleeves. Arleen was pouring the coffee. He sat down at the table. Her back was to him and there was an odd, tense line to her shoulders.

"What's the matter?" he asked.

"Nothing." She brought him his coffee, setting it on the table. Her eyes met his a moment, dropped to the floor. Somehow it made him think of Nita. Could Arleen know? Of course. George had been at the Black Jack last night. Brian was touched with a furtive guilt, and that was strange because Arleen had never made him feel guilty before. She had accepted his amours realistically. It was the thing he had always admired about her, the thing that made their relationship so unique.

"A new role for you," he said.

Her back was still turned, but he could see her

head lift. "I won't judge you, Brian. I refuse to judge you."

He smiled. "How about being jealous?"

She bowed her head, voice small and tight. "No."

This was reminiscent of the last time he had seen her here, the same strange mood, so foreign to their relationship. Only it was stronger now, clearer. He rose and stood behind her, hands on her arms. Her glossy black hair had a perfumed scent.

"I don't do it to hurt you, Arleen."

Her head bowed more deeply. "I know . . . I know."

"When did it change?"

"I don't know. I thought I could play the game. I guess the joke's over."

What she wanted was clear now. Solid ground, yes or no, mine completely or not at all. And yet she wouldn't put words to it. They understood each other too well for that. How many others had he left at this point? He'd lost count. Except that he'd always been able to exit laughing before. There was no flippancy in him now.

She pulled free of his hands, took a step away, and turned. She was arched stiffly against the sink, lips compressed. She had been close to tears but it was gone now; she had control of herself again.

"I'm sorry," she said. "Drink your coffee."

He took the cup and went back to the table. She stood watching him, eyes dull, lifeless. He felt stiff with her now, awkward. It was a familiar moment but it had never been so painful. He drank half the cup and then stood up. He would have kissed her good-by before. A laughing, teasing kiss or a thing of frank, full passion.

"I'd better go," he said. She did not answer. He went into the bedroom for his coat. Slipping into it, he went back past the kitchen door. She still stood at the sink. He stopped a moment. "Things change," he said. "Maybe you'll feel different in a few days."

"Sure." She smiled, stiffly. "Maybe I'll feel different."

6

Down the street, he unhitched his Steeldust at the rack and stepped aboard. He glanced once at the window's above. The end of an episode. Why should it bother him? It never had before. Perhaps because it went back so far, with Arleen. Perhaps because he had thought it would never come to this, with them. It all seemed a part of the shaking-up his life had taken these last weeks. Tiger's death seemed to have thrown everything out of joint. . . .

He got back to the Double Bit near dusk, stripped the Steeldust and turned it into the corral. Robles' two saddle horses were not there. He hurried to the house, a dark premonition growing within him. Pinto was in the kitchen, peeling potatoes. The crippled cook was used to Brian's escapades and greeted him as if he had just come in from an hour's ride.

"Afternoon, Brian. How about a hair of the dog."

"The ride back took care of that, thanks," Brian said. He hesitated, then asked, "Where's Robles?"

Pinto stripped a long peeling carefully off a potato. "Gone."

It was the tone of his voice, more than anything else, that told Brian the story. Slowly he wheeled, aware of Pinto raising his head to look, and walked down the hall to the living-room. It felt like the bottom was gone from his belly. It seemed to put the stamp of utter finality on his defeat of the preceding days. Robles had given him his chance. He had failed to measure up. His wild drunk in town had finished it. Hearing of it, Robles had known how complete was his failure and had left for good. For a moment he resented Robles for not giving him more time, more of a chance. Then he knew how wrong that was. The Indian had given him a lifetime. What had happened after Tiger's death was merely a culmination. Brian went to Tiger's big hide-seated chair by the fireplace and sank into it.

Yet the resentment would not leave him. The old Indian's action was too much like Tiger's constant nagging. Memory of Tiger always brought its dull grief; but with it were the bleak recollections of their old clashes. Hadn't he left that behind with Tiger's death? What right did the others have to judge him? Robles or Wolffe or Pa Gillette or any of them. If he didn't measure up to their standards, the hell with them. It was his life and, now more than ever, he would live it as he saw fit. With Tiger gone he was answerable to no one but himself, and it was going to stay that way.

A week later he received an invitation to a party at Ford Tarrant's. It was a glittering affair, with most of the unattached young women in the county there. It helped him take his mind off Tiger and it provided the impetus that returned him to the scapegrace existence he had known before Tiger's death.

Through the winter months, time gradually healed his grief over Tiger's loss. Little by little his carefree humor returned; little by little he slipped back into the familiar patterns of life.

He saw Arleen once in a while but the stiffness was still between them. The constant round of Christmas parties during December gave him little time to think about it. In the early part of the year he began giving affairs of his own at the Double Bit. All the questions and doubts of a few months before were submerged in a frantic whirl that left him little time for self-doubt. When Brian wasn't spending time in the higher social echelons he was carousing with his more disreputable cronies in town. He was playing the gay young bachelor to the hilt and it seemed sufficient.

That was the way things stood on the day early in May when he got word that George Wolffe wanted to see him in town. There had been a lull in things for the past few days and he welcomed a chance to go into Apache Wells. His Steeldust was being re-shod and he took the spring buggy with the scarlet bed and the bright yellow wheels.

It was good to ride into your home town that way. Good to smell the hot spring dust stirred up by your buggy wheels. Good to know there would be a friend on every corner, a bottle and a game waiting at the Black Jack, a dozen of the prettiest girls in Arizona to choose from when you got tired of cards. And the first friend to appear was Charlie Casket, stepping from the Café. There was a deck of cards in his hand, and Brian waved at him, expecting the old salute: "Pick a card, Brian."

But it didn't come. Casket stared at him blankly, holding the cards in one pale hand, neither nodding nor acknowledging the greeting. Farther on, it was the barber, standing in his doorway. Brian waited for the traditional greeting: "Looks like a shave this morning, Mr. Sheridan."

It didn't come. The barber didn't open his mouth. He stared at Brian with a strained, pale look to his face. When Brian was past he saw the man turn into his shop and speak to someone inside.

It made Brian pull his team down to a walk. The hot street ahead of him was empty save for a few forlorn cow-ponies stamping at the tie-racks. The silence of the town was like a pressure, cottony, waiting. The white dust sifted from beneath his wheels and settled like cornstarch on his coat. He pulled up before the feed store, and his eyes lifted to the windows above. Arleen's windows. He was brushed by a sense of loneliness.

There had been a dozen girls, since then. Why did they all seem so shallow?

With a curse, he shook the mood off and started to climb from his buggy. At the same time the banker's kid cut around a corner and ran toward the buggy. His eyes were round as silver dollars and there was fear on his white face. The boy caught the side of the buggy with a freckled hand.

"The Gillettes are in town," he panted. "They're lookin' for you and they've all got their guns."

Brian frowned sharply at the boy, then pulled a quarter from his pocket and flipped it to him. "Thanks, Dee. You better go home now."

Brian tried to shake his apprehension off. What the hell was wrong? He stepped out of the buggy, winding the reins around the whipstock. He had acquired a taste for bottle-green frock coats and wore a different hat for every day in the week. This was his Wednesday Stetson, bone-white and fresh-blocked, the one he always wore with his white silk cravat and bench-made boots of red Morocco. As he stepped up to the side-walk he saw three people come out of Jess Miller's Mercantile directly across the street. It was Pa Gillette and his two sons, Cameron and Asa. Their faces were white and set.

"Morning, Gillette," Brian smiled. "Your beef getting fatter on that new forty?"

There was no answer. Sweat glistened in the

deep channels of Pa Gillette's face and his mouth was narrow as a scar.

Behind him, moving ponderously as the mules he drove, came Cameron, an immense blond man with hair like straw thatching. Asa, the youngest son, brought up the rear, a nervous, driven boy with hollow cheeks and feverish eyes. Brian felt his face tighten as they stopped in front of him and stood there, staring at him in silence. Then Pa Gillette said:

"Guess you'll be the richest man in Gila County, now."

Brian frowned at him. "How do you mean?"

"Asa wanted to shoot you," Pa said. Anger shook his voice. "I told him they'd hang us for that."

"They can't hang us for whipping the hell out of you," Asa said.

Sudden anger cut through Brian. "What the hell for? I don't know what you're talking about, Pa."

"Morton Forge was always getting into some kind of trouble," Pa Gillette said thickly. "When you foreclosed on him, I thought maybe you was in the right. I even kept quiet when you shut down Partridge's outfit. He wanted to get up a bunch of us and burn you out. He said you was a damn octopus, eating us up. I wouldn't believe him. But you was just stringing us along till you really had us over a barrel, wasn't you? Tellin' us you wouldn't call in the note if we let it lapse a few months. Letting us stretch out so thin we

94

couldn't ever get back."

"Are you saying —"

"You know what happened," Pa almost shouted. He hooked Sheridan's coat with one hand, pulling him up on his toes. His voice broke with his rage and his eyes were blazing. "Your foreman was with the deputy sheriff when he brought the notice this morning."

Brian grabbed the man's arm, trying to twist free. "Let go, Pa. I didn't send the law out."

Still holding his coat, Pa shoved Brian back so hard he had to stumble against the wall of the building to retain his feet. "You can stand there and say that?" Pa shouted in his face. "An hour ago Cline's deputy was on my door-stoop and that damn Latigo with him."

"But I didn't send him!" Brian was shouting in a hot anger of his own now. He got purchase against the wall and thrust all his weight into Pa, shoving him back off balance and tearing free at the same time. He heard his coat rip. Pa tried to come back in at him, but Sheridan twisted free.

"Don't let him get away," Asa shouted.

Brian had a blurred impression of Cameron coming into him. He tried to dodge aside. But the man's great body smashed him back against the wall. He saw Cameron pull back a rope-scarred fist. Saw Pa Gillette lunging back in from the other side. Knew he'd be finished if they both caught him there.

He dropped to his knees as Cameron struck. The man's fist cracked into the wall above

Brian's descending head. Then he drove outward against the man, waist-high. It carried Cameron across the sidewalk and he pitched off the curb with Brian sprawling out on top of him.

He tried to roll off Cameron but both Pa and Asa lit on him from behind. He went back down beneath a fury of blows and kicks. Stunned by it, he had a blurred vision of a booted leg, and twisted around to catch it and throw his weight against it. This toppled Pa back into Asa and both of them went down.

Brian went right with them. He saw Asa's face before him as the man tried to twist free and rise. He smashed it square with all his weight behind the blow. Blood spurted and Asa was jerked backward to hit flat on his back against the street.

Brian was still partly on top of Pa. The elder Gillette twisted up into him, jamming a knee into the crotch. The pain of it made Brian double helplessly over on the man. Pa clawed at him, trying to get out from beneath. In desperation, Brian pawed for some handhold. His fingers found Pa's hair. Pa clawed at his eyes and tried to knee him again. Face still twisted with pain from that first knee, Brian slammed Pa's head against the ground. He was dimly aware of Asa rolling over, face whipped by rage.

"He's killin' Pa," Asa bawled. There was no reason left in the wild tone of his voice. Hot rage twisting his face, he went for his gun.

Brian let go of Pa's hair, rising up on the man,

filled with the helplessness of knowing what was coming and being utterly unable to stop it. Asa's gun was clear out before Estelle Gillette's figure blocked him off, jumping down into the street.

"You can't kill him in cold blood, Asa!" she cried.

Brian saw Asa jump to his feet, trying to lunge aside. But she threw herself into him, grabbing for the gun arm and hanging on, fighting with him till he finally stopped.

Brian tried to get up off the half-conscious Pa, but he was too drained to gain his feet. He had to crawl to the curb and hoist himself to a sitting position. The air passed in and out of him in great, broken gusts. Each breath was stabbing pain. He thought for a long while that he was going to be sick. At last, with a great effort, he lifted his head, to see Estelle Gillette still standing in front of Asa, her head turned over one shoulder to look at Sheridan.

"Thanks, Estelle," he said. "I think Asa really meant to kill me."

"Nobody would have been killed," George Wolffe said, from behind Sheridan. "Unless it was Asa."

Sheridan turned to see Wolffe standing by the bank door, a gun in his hand. His square face was Indian-dark with anger, beneath a flat-topped black hat, and his eyes were fixing their black intensity on Asa Gillette.

"I heard the commotion from my office," he told Brian. "I wish I could've gotten here sooner."

Brian winced as his grin pulled at cut lips. "I'll never leave lather in your shaving mug again, George. Where does a lawyer get off packing a smoke pole that big?"

Wolffe looked down at the huge Frontier Colt he held, and then raised his eyes again, unsmiling. Estelle had finally turned from her brother now. Her cheeks were flushed and her round young breasts swelled against her calico dress with every panting breath she took. But her lips settled into a full, almost pouting shape again as she regained her composure.

Cameron was on his feet, shaking his straw-thatched head from side to side like a bull with blow-flies. Pa's whole face was still squinted up with pain, but not enough to obscure the anger glittering in his sun-faded eyes.

"This ain't the finish," he said. His voice was guttural with rage and frustration. "You better stay indoors after this, Sheridan. You'll be taking your life in your hands to put one foot outside. There won't be a road safe for you to ride in all Arizona."

He turned and stalked off, gesturing for his clan to follow. Cameron and Asa followed, and it left only Estelle, standing in the street, staring at Brian with tortured eyes. He got shakily to his feet, holding out one hand.

"Estelle, you don't believe — ?"

She regarded him without answering. He couldn't tell whether it was hate in her eyes, or pity. Then she turned and left. Brian watched her go down the street after her family. At last Brian turned to go upstairs with Wolffe. At the stairway he grew so dizzy he had to lean against the rail. His face was putty-colored.

"You're really out of shape," George Wolffe said. "Little fight like that."

Sheridan laughed shakily. "Have to get in some more riding, I guess."

"I'm sorry about the girl."

"They come and go."

"I thought you were really interested in Estelle."

Sheridan glanced at him, seeing a sharp calculation in his eyes. "You manage my money, George," he said. "I'll take care of my love life." He turned squarely to Wolffe. "That was sort of a dirty deal, wasn't it? Tiger had given them his word we wouldn't push that note."

"They had no proof, Brian. How can we do business that way?"

"Pa said something about Forge and Partridge," Brian said. "Did you foreclose on them too?"

"They were six months behind on their notes. Claimed Tiger had made a verbal agreement with them too. I told you how this thing would get out of hand if we let the Gillettes get away with it."

"But I gave Pa Gillette my word too. Tiger made Sheridan a name anybody could trust, George. I've got to straighten this out."

George put a hand on his shoulder. "Simmer

down, Brian. You couldn't get within a mile of the Gillettes now, anyway. This is all a part of those politics you don't want to get involved in. For several years Pa Gillette has been the leader of the Salt River bunch. Tiger thought he'd won them over with his loans and his help. But you can't pull the little man and the big man together that easy. The Salt Rivers would still drag you down if they could. It's one of the reasons I asked you in today. We're having a meeting and I wanted you to see the truth."

The Gillettes' hatred had shaken Brian. Could he really be this blind to what lay beneath the surface of the town? He felt confused, subdued.

Ford Tarrant galloped down Cochise from the east end of town on a handsome, sweat-shiny Appaloosa. He pulled to a flourishing halt, grinning down at them. "Looks like you finally collared the prodigal, George. Brian going to join us?"

"Only if it's at the Black Jack," Brian said.

"No," Wolffe said sharply. "It'll only end up with another game. You dropped five hundred dollars to Casket last week."

"Don't nag, George."

"But you're getting in too deep, Brian."

Tarrant swung off his horse, beating dust from his tailored cutaway. "Indulge the young cock, George. It's obviously the only way you can interest him in the more serious aspects of life."

Grudgingly Wolffe gave in, and they went to the saloon. At his usual table sat Nacho, glazed sombrero tilted precariously back on his narrow black head, a corn shuck cigarette dangling from his slack mouth. He was playing black jack with Casket but when he saw Brian he turned to hail him. Brian saw the tarnished deputy's badge winking on one lapel of his greasy charro jacket.

"I knew the long arm would get you one way or the other," Brian said.

Nacho polished the star proudly with a palm. "How you like? It was me help Latigo foreclose on the Gillettes."

Brian stopped. "You?"

"Sure. Sheriff Cline had to go down to the county line after some Apaches jumping reservation. Nobody left to serve the eviction notice official. He deputize me before he leave."

Brian shook his head. "I wish you hadn't done that."

Nacho laughed heartily. "Listen to him. Does that sound like the son of Tiger Sheridan? Tiger would have gone to the Gillette place himself, tear them apart one by one, and throw them off the land piece by piece. I myself saw Tiger turn a stampede once with nothing but a lighted match. It was a night like coal, and here they come, and he didn't have no horse or nothing —"

"You couldn't of seen him," one of the Double Bit hands said. "That happened before you were born."

"I don't even think it happened," the barman said, cleaning a glass. "It can't be done. Just one of those things you hear about Tiger Sheridan."

Nacho turned on the barman. "But it can be done, Jigger. The thing animals fear mos' is fire. Even a little flame like that."

Jigger put his tongue in one cheek and winked broadly at Sheridan, asking Nacho, "Would you like to try it?"

The deputy arched his chest, pounding on it. "Jus' give me the stampede. I show you."

"Let's go," whooped one of the Double Bit hands. "I got just the cattle for you."

It was the old, good-natured ragging Sheridan had heard a hundred times, and he could not help feeling a return of his humor. "All right," he said. "Joke's over. If Tiger was here he'd throw you all out in the street for doubting that story."

Charlie Casket sat at one of the rear tables, his face gaunt and hollow-eyed in the dim light. "Pick a card, Brian."

Brian went through the routine with him, picking a queen of hearts, shuffling, holding the deck out to the gambler. Casket picked a card out, held it face up.

"Queen of Hearts," Wolffe said wonderingly.

"Uncanny, Charlie," Sheridan said, sinking down into a chair. He held up a finger at the barman. "Bring the bottle, Jigger."

Brian had downed several drinks when Jess Miller came into the saloon, hurrying, round face ruddy and shining with perspiration. He greeted them all absently, pulling a chair up.

"Heard you had a fight with the Gillettes," he

told Brian. "You must be convinced they're —"

"Forget it, Jess," Wolffe said.

The storekeeper looked at Wolffe in surprise. Then something fluttered through his eyes. "Sorry, Brian. Guess it isn't the happiest subject."

"Hardly," Brian said. He looked at Wolffe. "All right. Who we going to put up for governor?"

Wolffe scowled, but Tarrant laughed, pulling a folded sheaf from his coat. "It's Mayor, Brian. We're circulating a petition to recall Mayor Prince. Pa Gillette got his Salt River bunch to block it. But with the Gillettes on the run the picture will be different."

Jess Miller poured Brian a drink, leaning forward confidingly. "You know how much weight the Sheridan name bears in this country. Your signature on the petition will draw the others like lilies."

Brian let whisky slide down his throat, oil and fire in one. "What's wrong with Mayor Prince?"

"Who do you think is pushing this franchise through for Arizona Mail and Freight," Tarrant said. "Prince's influence goes through the council here and straight into the state capitol. With a railroad in Apache Wells, the Salt River bunch will be able to handle ten times the beef they do now."

Nacho rolled a cigarette. "Is so, Brian. Only reason we've been able to keep the Salt Rivers from running bigger drives is that Alta is so far away, and our people own most of the water along the route."

"Mayor Prince is a Salt River man," Tarrant said. "You can't afford to let him get us over a barrel, Brian. Make this a shipping point, the Salt Rivers can handle more beef. The more beef they handle, the bigger they get. Let 'em get big enough and they'll squeeze us out. We've got to stop them before they begin. We've got proof that Prince was bribed by the railroad to push this franchise through, and we're going to recall him for it."

"What kind of proof?"

"Councilman Lewis overheard a division superintendent for Arizona Mail offer Prince a cut of the freight rates between here and Alta —"

"Isn't that sort of flimsy evidence?"

"It'll stand up in court if we don't let the Salt Rivers get any stronger," Tarrant said. "Now you promised me you'd sign the recall petition at the party the other night."

Brian took another long drink, squinting ruefully. "After ten o'clock things got sort of hazy."

Wolffe's voice was barely a murmur. "Now don't tell me you can't remember that either?"

Sheridan looked at him for help. "Did I promise, George?"

"It was your word you were so worried about breaking a few minutes ago," Wolffe said.

Brian tried to focus his eyes. Wolffe seemed blurred. Miller poured him another drink. Brian chuckled affectionately at the cherubic little merchant.

"If I gave my word, I'll sign," Brian grinned. "I feel too good to hold up a game. Anybody got a pen?"

Jigger brought a pen and ink. While Brian signed, Casket began to deal the cards, and they plunged into the game. Brian lost all sense of time. It was the smoke-filled room and the soft laughter of men and the slap of cards and losing a pot or winning it and the cards becoming more and more blurred until he shoved his chair back, shaking his head and staring around the room. Wolffe was sitting at another table, a candle at his elbow, immersed in one of his law books.

"Anybody got the time?" Sheridan asked.

Tarrant yawned, looking at his watch. "Two o'clock."

Brian chuckled tipsily. "Man's drunk, he'd better quit. How much you owe me, Charlie?"

"You owe me," Casket said. "Eight hundred dollars."

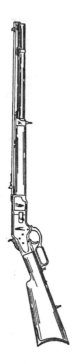

7

A week after the fight with the Gillettes, Brian gave another of his innumerable parties. By now he had admitted to himself that he was missing Arleen. He had thought he could dismiss her as easily from his life as he had a dozen others. But he had been wrong. He was nagged by a sense of loss that could not be buried in the whirl of parties. His relationship with Arleen had been a unique compound of comfortable understanding and strange excitement — and he had been unable to find its counterpart in any of the dozen girls he had been with this last year. And so, though he didn't believe she would come, he sent an invitation to Arleen and George anyway.

At eight o'clock on the appointed evening Juanita tapped on Brian's door with news that the first guests were arriving. He emerged from his room, resplendent in a boiled shirt, bottle-green scissortail and cream-colored kerseymere pants. He had brought an orchestra by special train to Alta, and to the Double Bit by stage. They were at one end of the huge living-room, already tuning up. Soft-footed Mexican servants were loading the tables with silver trays of canapés and hors d'oeuvres prepared by the chef who had accompanied the orchestra from Santa Fe. The light of the countless candles reflected against the cut glass and silverware on the tables, filling the room with a brilliant glitter.

Ford Tarrant was at the door with Opal Manners, a daughter of one of the big ranchers on the Rim. As a servant took their wraps, Ford spoke confidentially to Brian.

"You'll be glad to know your name on that petition did the trick, Brian."

"Petition?"

"To recall Mayor Prince. We won't have enough paper to handle all the signatures."

Brian smiled. "Tell you the truth, I'd forgotten."

Tarrant grinned and shook his head helplessly. Opal took his arm. "It's against the law to talk politics at Brian's parties. Let's take advantage of that orchestra."

As more and more couples arrived, the dance floor filled up and the bar became crowded. A last rig pulled up in the outer darkness and in a moment George Wolffe and his sister appeared at the door. Indian-dark, black-haired, black-eyed, Arleen wore a clinging gown of shimmering gold satin that accented every curve. Brian knew how long she must have scrimped and saved to get such a dress on the slender budget her brother allowed. He felt a little breathless, strangely awkward before her. Their greetings were stiff and Brian felt a flush creep up his neck.

"Did you have to import that orchestra?" Wolffe said. "You must realize what all this is doing to your accounts."

"They're in capable hands," Brian said.

"You've got to come in and go over the books with me again, Brian. I can't have you squandering your whole fortune."

Brian chuckled at him. "I like you, George, but you should take life more seriously. Why not have a drink at the bar and leave Arleen and me alone?"

Scowling, George left them. Brian asked Arleen to dance. She nodded and he swung her onto the floor. She would not let him hold her as closely as before. They swung around in a sedate waltz and the awkwardness was there again.

"I understand Ford's been squiring you around," he said.

"Jealous?"

"Very."

His usual glibness was gone. Her bare shoulders gleamed whitely and the musky perfume of her was all around him. His temples throbbed faintly and there was a dryness at the roof of his mouth. Had he really forgotten how much she excited him? The enigmatic smile was still on her lips, like a wall between them.

"Let's try the champagne," he said. "I feel like something should be shaken loose."

She seemed to relax a little, laughing softly.

They drank and then danced some more. It was a little better. But the barrier was still there. All through dinner it was still there. It filled him with a sense of frustration and after the meal he drank too much. There was an exchange of partners in the dancing but at last he got around to Arleen again. He went through half the dance and then guided her toward a rear door.

"How about a walk? It's hot in here."

They drifted into the flagstoned patio. At the rear a red-roofed well and a circle of greening willows screened them from the house. They stopped here and he stood close. She turned a shoulder to him, cool, distant.

"What shall we talk about, Brian? Politics?"

"You know what I want to talk about."

"Let's not embarrass each other, Brian. Isn't that over?"

It blocked him. "All right," he said angrily. "I don't know a damn thing about politics. What do you know?"

Her face was hidden from him. "Only what I hear. The talk around town is that you plan to let the Gillettes stay on their land."

"I gave my word. I'm going out to see them tomorrow."

"You shouldn't."

He said, half jokingly, "George can't convince me, so they throw in the reserves."

For a moment her face went taut. Then she said, "Estelle will be very grateful."

There was a thin sound to her voice, a feline sound. For a moment he couldn't believe it. Then he had to smile.

"This is a new twist. You know I never got anywhere with her."

"Maybe this will help."

"Arleen — I'm not going out there for that."

"Pa Gillette's the only one strong enough to hold the Salt Rivers together," Arleen said. "Let him stay and you're keeping alive the very bunch that wants to pull you down. You'd only be that foolish if a girl was involved."

"She isn't involved. How can I convince you?"

"By not going out there."

"Now you're being crazy. I'm sick of the whole situation. I can't go back on my word to Pa Gillette. That's all there is to it. George and Ford have been on my neck about it for a week. I won't take it from you, too —"

He broke of at the expression on her face. Her lips were slack, drooping, tears sparkled in her wide eyes. She was closer to crying than he had ever seen her before. He put his hands on her bare arms.

"Arleen, I didn't mean it that way. I —"

She seemed to sway closer. With an inarticulate sound he took her roughly into his arms and kissed her. It was hard, bruising contact, holding pain and passion together. Yet she did not shrink from it. The length of her soft body molded to him, trembling, and her arms locked about his neck. The world rocked and the pound of his

110

temples ran through his whole body. Her mouth slid off his and she spoke in a gasping, broken little voice.

"I guess it was silly of me . . . but a woman can't think straight when . . . when . . ."

He waited for her to finish. Finally he pulled back, taking her face in his hands. *When she's in love.* He wanted her to say it. *When she's in love.* But she didn't have to. Her eyes opened, out of focus, a little glazed. And the answer was there.

His voice shook. "Arleen. It's what I wanted to tell you when we first came out here. I've missed you. It took our bust-up to make me realize how much you meant. I guess it all came together tonight."

Her eyes opened wider. Her lips parted expectantly. His need of her was no longer the nagging, indefinable loneliness he had felt these last months. It was vivid, passionate, more complete a want than he'd ever known for a woman. Before he realized it, he was putting it into words.

"You said you couldn't play the game any more. I guess I can't either. I want you to marry me, Arleen."

"Brian . . . Brian . . ."

It left her on a little sigh. She came into his arms again, face buried against the side of his neck this time. He held her tight.

"We'll announce it tonight," he said. "You'll be a June bride. The biggest wedding this country ever saw —"

"Brian, wait."

Her voice sounded strange, tight. She pulled free and turned away, walking to the well. He understood her hesitation, the doubt that had always been there with her, with all of them.

He followed and stood behind her. "A man with a wife's got to settle down, Arleen. It'll be different. You've got my word."

"And you won't go out to the Gillettes'?"

"Arleen, that hasn't got anything to do with us."

"Hasn't it?"

"What kind of a man do you think I am? I just asked you to marry me. Do you think I'd turn around and —"

"Then you aren't going out there?"

Anger made his voice shake. "I am. I gave my word. It has nothing to do with Estelle. I —"

"Brian — Brian —"

Her voice stopped him. He realized he had been close to shouting. He felt like a fool. His face was hot and his hands were clenched and he felt like a fool. She turned to him, taking his lapels.

"Forgive me," she said. She wasn't looking at him. "Maybe it isn't all Estelle, Brian. I can't help being afraid for you."

"Afraid?"

"Don't you remember what Pa Gillette told you in town, after the fight?"

His anger faded, as he recalled Pa Gillette's

threat. "He was mad, Arleen. He couldn't mean it."

She shook her head. "All right. Let's not talk about it any more."

"I'm willing. All I want to talk about is us."

Her face tilted up sharply. "Give me a little time, Brian. I've got to think. You must realize how abrupt it was, how completely unexpected."

"It was just having you near again, realizing at last what I really wanted." He paused, awkwardly. He felt helpless, with the situation out of his control. He had been so sure this was what she wanted. He said, "Take all the time you need, Arleen. I want both of us to be sure."

She seemed about to speak again. Then she turned and started back toward the house and he followed, taking her arm. At the door he was met by Latigo. Dust chalked the heavy-framed man's jacket and Levis. Sweat lay greasily in the grooves of his face and the lather of a hard-ridden horse was on his boots. He said he wanted to see Brian a moment. Arleen excused herself. Brian looked after her, his mind only half on what Latigo was saying.

"We're about finished with calf roundup," Latigo said. "I wanted you to see the tally books."

Brian shook his head impatiently. "Wolffe will take care of it."

"I can't find him. Somebody's got to go over these with me, Brian. We're bled white on the young stuff. As things stand we won't have any-thing for a trail herd this fall."

"Damn it, Latigo. Can't you see I'm busy? Come back tomorrow."

Brian tried to brush by him but Latigo caught his arm. "Look, Brian, I rode all the way in here from the roundup just to —"

"Take your hands off me!"

For a moment longer Latigo held him, anger smoldering in his heavy-lidded eyes. Finally he let his hand slide off. The shadows seemed to deepen in the gaunt hollows beneath his blunt cheekbones.

"Don't talk that way to me, Brian. You ain't Tiger."

Brian felt his whole body stiffen with rage. Then he realized what a fool he was being and shook his head, passing a hand over his eyes.

"Sorry, Latigo. Everything seems wrong tonight. I've had too much to drink or some-thing. I'll find Wolffe for you. He'll settle this."

There was no relenting in Latigo's dust-grimed face. His eyes still smoldered with anger as Brian turned inside. He found Wolffe, told him about the foreman, then went to the punch bowl for another drink. But that didn't remove his oppression. He had the sense of something wrong, out of joint. Was it Arleen's hesitation? Or their strange clash over Estelle? Was it logical that she should be so jealous of Estelle? He tried to dismiss it. Who could tell what lay in a woman's mind? Not enough young stuff for the trail herd. That wasn't right either, somehow. Was it the rustling again? He wished these things didn't always come up when he was drunk.

8

A brazen sun beat down against
the trackless floor of Skeleton Canyon until the heat waves rising
from the parched sand formed a
buttery haze in the rock-walled
gorge. There was no sound except
the fretting crackle of wind
through baking creosote bushes.
The sweat lay like oil on the shoulders of Brian's
Steeldust stallion and dripped steadily from
beneath his hat brim to make clammy tracks in
the dust-caked mask of his face.

The party the night before had lasted into the
wee hours and Brian was still half-sick from his
hangover. In a vile mood, he had started out to
the Gillettes'. Wolffe had told him that they were
staying on their property in defiance of the
foreclosure. The next move would be for the
sheriff to evict them again and post a deputy on
the place.

Brian's horse balked, whinnying sharply. He
pulled it in, staring at its twitching ears. He
turned his squinted eyes up to the glittering
rimrock of the canyon. Somehow it made him
think of what Arleen had said last night about Pa

Gillette's threat: "There won't be a road safe for you to ride in all Arizona."

He shook his head angrily. He was being stupid. He gigged the horse on, wiping sweat from his face. Heat devils danced before his eyes. A sharp pain ran through his temples. He had been out this way before, but hadn't remembered it was such a grueling ride.

Approaching a sharp turn, the horse began to fiddle again. Brian began to pull the reins. He was filled with an with an insidious reluctance to round the turn. He looked about him again. Glaring sand in the bottom, blinding rim of red rock high above. Nothing else.

He put heels to the nervous horse and forced it into a canter. They wheeled around the turn and the canyon narrowed ahead. He was thinking of Arleen again and of his proposal last night. It had been almost as great a surprise to him as it had been to her. He certainly hadn't planned it when he had invited her. Yet at the time he had been more certain of his need for her than he'd ever been of anything.

And now?

He grimaced. Maybe doubt was always a part of the morning after. Was a man ever sure of anything when it came to a woman? Maybe only when she was in his arms. And maybe that was all that mattered —

His shadowy thoughts were shattered by the roaring crack of a gun from above. Its echoes rocked the gorge and Brian saw chips kicked out of a rock a foot to his right.

The horse reared up, pitching him off its rump. He hit heavily and flopped over on his belly. There were shooting pains through his right leg and that whole side of his body seemed numb. Desperately he crawled on his belly through the sand to the partial protection of the boulder. He was sweating and trembling from shock. Sprawled in the sand, he pulled his Bisley. He squinted his eyes against the sun searching the rimrock. The strata of sandstone and shale up there gleamed crimson in the sunlight. He could see nothing. His horse was gone, out of sight and out of earshot. Then there was the glitter up on a ridge like sunlight on metal. He realized how exposed he was here. The glitter had come from across the canyon, and he had to cross to that side.

Since they had not shot again that could mean they were getting into position. It gave him a small chance. His right leg was no longer numb, though the pain was still there. He rose to his knees, throwing himself into a lunging run across the sandy floor. He dropped behind the protection of a rock on the other side, surprised that there had been no shot. Then he began the climb to the rimrock.

It was a treacherous, exhausting struggle up to the top, squeezing through rocky fissures, scrambling laterally across the face of lose talus slopes. He reached a ledge halfway up and sank exhausted against a sun-baked rock. It seemed he could not get enough air. He was so dizzy from the exertion that he could not focus his eyes. Why should he be this played out? It hadn't been that hard a climb.

Still dizzy and panting he pulled himself up for the rest of it. He reached the top so drained he had to sprawl on his belly behind the shelter of a lava uplift, unable to get to his feet. Finally he crawled to hands and knees, looking over the uplift to see that he was on an immense plateau that ran northward beyond sight. He crouched there until he saw a vague movement a few hundred yards down the rim of the canyon. He crawled on hands and knees out of the lava, using jagged rocks and twisted junipers for cover. He was within fifty yards of the spot when a man suddenly appeared, working his way along the rim of the canyon. It happened so fast that Sheridan could not make out who it was.

All he saw was the dim form rising suddenly from behind a black clump of creosote, the glitter of sun on metal again. He jumped to his feet in his excitement, firing the first shot. His bullet kicked sand up in front of the man, obscuring him even more.

Sheridan ran thoughtlessly toward him, firing again and again. There was a shout and the man disappeared. Sheridan kept running until he reached the edge of a gully that ran back into the plateau from the rim of the canyon. He was going so fast he couldn't stop himself from running over onto the steep slope of the gully. He danced wildly to keep his feet as he slid down through the shale. He hit the bottom at a stumbling run with a vague impression of motion ahead of him where the gully made a turn. He fired again, twice, and then his hammer clicked on an empty chamber.

He brought himself up short, panting, dizzy again, realizing how foolish he had been, running in on the man this way. Like some fool kid with buck fever. Again he sought the cover of a jagged rock and crouched there on one knee, reloading his gun. His hands were shaking so badly he could hardly punch the shells from their chambers. Finally he got it reloaded and began to work his way down the canyon again. He reached the turn and moved around it with his gun cocked.

The gully pinched off here and he could see the prints of a horse in its sandy bottom. Brian halted, defeat dragging at his shoulders, as he realized the man was gone. Finally Brian turned and walked back through the gully till he reached the rim of Skeleton Canyon. His exhaustion forced him to admit at last how weak and soft these last years of rich living had left him and he wondered seriously if he had the strength to make it alive out of this desert on foot.

It was night when Brian reached the Double Bit. The featherweight soles of his bench-made boots had been cut to ribbons hours ago by the sharp rocks of the desert; his feet were swollen so badly that each step was an agony. His tattered clothes hung slack and dust-filled on his stumbling body and he went to his knees once under the row of poplars before finally gaining the porch. His strange, stumbling figure startled the horses hitched at the cottonwood rack and they began whinnying and pulling at their reins. This must have been heard from inside for the door was swung wide. In the lamplight streaming out Brian saw Arleen standing there, lustrous black hair framing the pale oval of her face.

"Brian!" she said sharply. Then she gathered up her full red skirts and came hurrying across the porch to keep him from falling. He sagged gratefully against the soft warmth of her body. He felt her stiffen.

"George —" she said. There was a strange, brittle tone to her voice. "Come and get him."

George Wolffe and Ford Tarrant were already coming out the door. They caught Brian under the arms. He was vaguely aware of Arleen stepping back, brushing the dust off her red dress.

"Somebody took a shot at me," Brian said, as they helped him through the door. "My horse spooked and threw me."

Tarrant helped lower Brian to the sofa and then stepped back, taking a long black cigar out and thrusting his portly belly forward expansively. "If I was mayor, things like this wouldn't happen. That damned Prince is letting our town fill up with riffraff —"

"Riffraff, hell," Wolffe said. "We all know who

did this. There were a dozen people who heard the Gillettes threaten Brian.

Arleen poured a drink from the decanter on the desk. Brian took it and downed it neat, seeing that Charlie Casket was in the living-room also. He sat in the big wing chair by the fireplace shuffling a pack of cards and had not offered to rise. He held the cards out, poker-faced.

"Take one?"

Brian started at him, too sick and beaten for clear thought. "What are you doing here, Charlie?"

"He thought you might like a little game tonight," Tarrant said. "Didn't know you'd gone out on that fool's errand to the Gillette's. Are you convinced now that the foreclosure's got to stick?"

Brian settled back in the chair. "I can't quite believe they'd do something so cold-blooded."

"Don't be a fool," Tarrant exploded. "You've got to put Pa Gillette out of the game. The Salt River bunch will fall apart without him. And we can't be sure of Prince's recall unless he loses their support. The whole thing stands or falls on this Gillette deal."

Brian looked at Wolffe. "And you were the one who foreclosed on the Gillettes."

"Damn it, Brian, it's for your own good," Wolffe said. "They try to kill you twice and you still can't see that. You're a big man. As long as that's true, men like Gillette and his crowd will be trying to pull you down. You've got to fight back."

Brian frowned at Tarrant. "You said if *you* were mayor. I thought you were putting Conners up against Prince on this recall petition."

Tarrant looked at his cigar. "Conners has backed down. I think the Salt River bunch reached him somehow."

"We nominated Tarrant at a special meeting today," Wolffe said. "Now, Brian, it's time you grew up and met your responsibilities. Give us your word you'll let that Gillette foreclosure stand. It's the only way we can protect ourselves."

Brian shook his head. "Not till I see the Gillettes."

"Brian's in no shape to talk politics," Arleen said. "Can't this all wait?"

Tarrant shook his head. "This has to be settled."

"Then you'll be here for hours," Arleen said. "I'll take the buckboard back to town, George. You can come in with Ford."

Wolffe nodded without looking at her. She sent Brian an oblique glance. He started to rise.

"No need to see me out," she said. "You're too shaky."

He sank back, smiling gratefully. Tarrant waited till she was out the front door before he spoke.

"You force us to do this, Brian," Tarrant said. "Will you come in the study?"

Frowning in puzzled apprehension, Brian dragged himself from the chair and followed him down the hall, with Casket and Wolffe behind. The study door was open and Latigo sat with one leg on the desk, a pile of tally books beside him. He was still in his dust-grayed jeans and red underwear.

"We might as well start with Casket," Tarrant said.

The gambler pulled a sheaf of papers from his pocket. "They're checks and I.O.U.'s, Brian." he said. "You'd be surprised how much you've lost to me in those card games over the last couple of years. It amounts to around thirty thousand dollars."

Brian felt hot anger well up in him at the implications. "You mean you've been saving those things —" He broke off, staring at Tarrant. "You have a motley collection on your payroll, Ford. We'll go to the bank tomorrow. I'll get the cash."

"Your personal account is overdrawn," Wolffe said. "I got the bank statement today."

"Then we'll get it from the business account."

"That well's dry too," Wolffe said, tapping a pile of papers on the desk. "With no money in your personal account, I had to put these through the business account. They're the bills for this year. Over fifty thousand dollars."

Brian wheeled on him. "There was more than that in the business account the last time I went over the books with you."

Wolffe shook his head. "You forget the parties. Last night cost over four thousand dollars. You've thrown a dozen of them this year already."

"Damn you —" Brian started to say they'd sell some stock. Then he sensed what Latigo was here for, and stared down at the beef books.

"I tried to you last night," Latigo said. "We've still got a herd, but it's all too young to ship for beef. You bled us white on three-year-olds to pay for that trip East last year."

"Then we'll sell the stuff right here," Brian said, desperation entering his voice. "Every man in Gila County would give his right arm for some Double Bit cattle."

"And pay you with a note," Tarrant said sarcastically. "Nobody has that kind of cash around here."

Brian looked helplessly at Wolffe, who shook his head. "You've gotten yourself into this hole, Brian."

"And you let me! You knew what they were up to!"

Wolffe flushed. "How many times did I try to stop you from having these parties, Brian, from gambling, from wasting your money on whims?"

"If Charlie presses these gambling debts, it'll ruin you," Tarrant said. "He'd have to slap an attachment on your property to get the money and it'd be around town in five minutes. You'd have a hundred creditors up here pounding your door. You wouldn't have the shirt left on your back."

Brian stared around the circle of their faces, physically sick with the realization of how they had used him.

"All you have to do is give us your word you'll let the Gillette foreclosure stand," Tarrant said. "And Charlie won't press these gambling debts."

Brian realized he was trembling with his anger. "Get out," he said.

"They didn't want to do it this way, Brian," Wolffe said. "You made them. It's for your own good, don't you realize that?"

Brian had not reacted to anger this violently in a long time. Face white with rage, he yanked open the desk drawer and whipped out the old Colt dragoon his father had always kept there.

"If the whole bunch of you snakes isn't out of here in one minute this is going off in somebody's face!"

9

There was nothing much Brian could do that night. He was too sick and too filled with frustrated rage to sleep much. He spent half the time pacing his room in his bathrobe, trying to figure a way out of this. At five he had the cook fix him black coffee and toast and then he was in the saddle on the way to the Gillettes'. This time he wore his Bisley and had a Winchester in the saddle boot. He did not take the Skeleton Canyon route but drove through the badlands north of the canyon.

It was mid-morning and already burning hot by the time he reached the Gillettes', beaten down by the ride. They had a little greasy sack outfit in the footslopes of the Apaches. He passed through a poor man's gate, with Sheriff Cline's notice tacked on one of the cottonwood poles, and rode warily in toward the adobe house and corrals. There was no stock in the corrals, however, and a strange quiet hung over everything. He rode up to the door, saw that it was ajar. He stepped down, went inside. The house was empty. The Gillettes had already left.

He went wearily back to his horse, seeing how everything was closing about him. The Salt River bunch were strung out along the river for many miles toward Tempe, and the next man down was Wirt Peters. He had once worked for Tarrant, but had struck out on his own, and had subsequently become a great friend of the Gillettes. Brian headed for his place, reaching it in the heat of midday, hoping Peters was not out on roundup.

The man was a bachelor, with a little two-room adobe set back in a gash between two ridges. He must have been out on near-by roundup, for his horse and the animals of his two Mexican hands stood channeled with sweat by the *ramada* under which the three men were eating. Peters rose as Brian rode in.

Brian drew rein before him, leaning out of the saddle. "Wirt, you seen the Gillettes?"

"I have not," Peters said.

"Cline evicted them," Brian said. "I've got to find them."

Raw anger exploded in Peters' voice. "What the hell you coming to me for? I ought to gun you off the place. Maybe you think you can foreclose on me too."

"I didn't even want to foreclose on them, Wirt. There's been a mistake. It goes for you too. For everybody I hold a note on. I could call those notes in if I wanted. But the name of Sheridan would never mean anything again in this land. I gave my word to Pa I wouldn't call in his note even if it went overdue. It's the same to you. Only I need your help. Can you give me any cash at all on what you owe? I'm in a hole, Peters."

The man studied his horse, spat into the dust. "You must be in a hole to beat yourself down thataway. I never seen you exert yourself beyond reaching for a drink in all your life. I can't give you any cash, Brian. This land don't leave a man anything."

Sheridan felt himself sink against the saddle. "How about Purdy?"

"His wife's had another baby. He didn't even have the money for the doctor."

Brian took a ragged breath. "All right. At least pass the word along to the Gillettes."

"I'll do that." The wind-wrinkles fanned out from Peters' quizzical eyes as he gazed up at Sheridan, his voice half mocking. "I always thought life was going to turn around and kick you in the teeth one of these days, Brian."

Brian rode the day out seeking the Gillettes and looking up the men who owed the Double Bit money. But everywhere it was the same story. He stayed that night with one of the Mexican families who had served his father in the early days, filled with the sick realization that he could not get any help out here. He hit Apache Wells the next day, dust-grayed and beaten out by the constant riding, and went first to Jess Miller's Mercantile. The store was a single big room in a frame building filled with the linty smell of fresh calico and the sick-sweet odor of blackstrap sorghum. Miller sat on a high stool back in the gloom, a pencil over his ear, his body humped over a ledger. Somehow he didn't look as cherubic or expansive as he had seemed at their parties. There was a pinched look to his face as he worked on the figures. Then he heard Brian's footfall and looked up sharply.

"Jess," Brian said. "You and I've been friends a long time —"

Miller took the pencil cautiously from his ear. "Yes, Brian?"

"I'll say it straight. I need a loan. We saw you through those first two rough years and I thought you might be willing to return the favor."

"I've only got a couple of hundred in the safe, Brian. That be enough?"

"It's got to be fifty or sixty thousand, Jess."

The man's eyes popped open. "Lord, Brian, you won't find that much money in all Apache Wells."

Brian leaned toward him. "I know what kind of money you've been pulling in, Jess, and I know you've got the cash. I'm asking you as a friend —"

"I can't do it, Brian." Something furtive went through the man's pale eyes. "You're wrong about my money. It's been a bad year for everybody. A man has to hang onto what little money he's got —"

Brian straightened slowly, as he saw how it was. "You do that," he said, at last, in a disgusted voice. "You just do that."

He walked out of the store at a savage stalk, halting on the sidewalk outside. But defeat was draining the anger from him. Miller had been his last bet. He knew that to go to Troy Hadley would be useless. The banker was too shrewd a business man to put money into a losing proposition. And it was a losing proposition. More and more Brian saw that.

The planks began to tremble and he turned to see Jim Murphy coming toward him. Murphy was a paunchy, middle-aged lawyer from Alta. He cleared his throat uncomfortably as he halted before Brian.

"Glad I found you, Brian. Just got in on the stage. Going up to your place. Glad I found you."

Brian tried to regain some of his old jauntiness. "What for, Jim? Trying to cut Wolffe out of some business?"

"Not that —" Murphy tugged at his collar, looking into the street. "Truth of the matter is, some bills you owe were put before the court at Alta. They got in touch with Wolffe and found out you can't meet payment. Truth of the matter is, I've been appointed receiver by the court."

"Receiver? I haven't declared bankruptcy yet."

"Wolffe did that for you. He has your power of attorney. Uh — we'll give you time to vacate the premises, of course. House goes up for auction the eighth."

131

Brian felt all the blood drain from his face. "They sure as hell didn't waste any time, did they?"

"Wolffe has the papers in his office, if you want to sign 'em." Murphy pulled at his sweat-drenched collar. "I don't like this any more'n you do, Brian."

Brian felt his shoulders sag. "I suppose not, Jim." He turned heavily and walked down to Wolffe's office. Wolffe sat before the big battered desk in the front room, writing something, and glanced up sharply as Sheridan entered. The dust-filmed windows washed out the strong sunlight till it lit Wolffe's face with a sallow tint, settling deep shadows in the strongly marked hollows of his heavy-boned face.

"It's like you to run out on your responsibilities," he said acidly. "I've looked high and low for you, Brian. They've got us backed against the wall."

"I should be mad as hell with you, George," Sheridan said. "But somehow I can't."

Wolffe leaned forward, fixing the disturbing intensity of his burning eyes on Sheridan's face. "How often did I try to stop that profligate spending of yours? It was you that got us into this hole. When I saw what Tarrant planned, what could I do? You can still save yourself if you'll play along with Tarrant. He can have Casket's suit withdrawn. He might even get Troy Hadley to loan you the money to take care of the other creditors that have started clamoring."

"All I have to do is go back on my word to Gillette," Brian said thinly.

"You can't look at it that way —"

"I do." Brian stared out the dusty window. "It's funny. I guess I've asked help from every friend I had. It's funny how different they look when you need help. I'm deadbust, George."

"You will be if you don't use your head."

"It makes a man think. I guess it's the first time I've really thought in all my life. When all your money's gone, when every friend you had runs out on you — all you have left is your word —"

"Brian —"

"That's all I have left of what Dad built here, Wolffe. But it's the greatest thing of them all. I'm not going to lose it too." He wheeled toward the man. "Murphy said you had some papers to sign. I suppose I might as well get it over with."

After he left Wolffe's office he seemed too drained to feel anger any more. Or defeat. Or anything. It seemed as if these last two days had used up his capacity for emotion. He was filled with a great apathy. He supposed part of it was a physical letdown after the endless hours of riding. Force of habit made him seek relief in a drink. His Steeldust was still hitched in front of the Mercantile, halfway between Wolffe's office and the Black Jack. As he turned to go to the saloon, he saw a man at the hitch-rack, untying the reins.

133

Brian started toward him at a hard walk. "That's my horse, Latigo."

"Not any more," the foreman said. "The receivers are up at your house, checking all the stock. This horse was missing."

Brian reached him, yanking the reins out of his callused hands. "It's my personal animal. They can't take a man's horse any more than they can take his pants."

Latigo's eyes grew heavy-lidded with insolence. "They gave me my orders. They won't be able to pay off all your debts with what they got. This horse is worth twenty-five hundred dollars. I'll take the reins."

"The hell you will!" Brian threw the rawhide lines over the stallion's head and swung around to toe the stirrup.

Latigo caught his shoulder and swung him back. Brian's foot was hung up in the stirrup and he knew he was going to fall anyway so he let his momentum pitch his body around into Latigo. It knocked the man back against the hitch-rack. The hip-high bar flipped Latigo helplessly backward onto the sidewalk. And Brian went on his face in the dirt, his foot still caught in the stirrup. The excited stallion reared up. Brian felt his boot tear free. At the same time, Latigo rolled over and gained his feet. His eyes were almost shut with rage. As Brian tried to rise, the foreman jumped right back over the rack at him.

Brian could not roll aside soon enough. He shouted with pain as Latigo's spike heels stabbed into his back and drove him down into the dirt. Latigo jumped off Brian and swung a kick at his face.

It made a bright explosion of pain in Brian's consciousness. He rolled away, hugging his arms around his head. He had a dim view of Latigo's legs churning toward him and knew another kick would finish him. He came to his knees and launched himself bodily at hip-height.

He plunged into Latigo and clamped his arms around the man, driving him backward. The foreman tripped on the curb and went down. Brian sprawled across him, dimly aware of men spilling out of the Black Jack, of a crowd gathering.

Brian tried to slam a blow at Latigo. The man blocked it and pitched him off. Brian rolled away, trying to gain his feet. He was reaching for air like a windsucker. When he got his feet under him his legs wobbled like a newborn calf's. How could he be so weak? He saw Latigo come up and lunge for him. He staggered backward, trying to set himself. The man shifted around before him and threw a blow. Brian put up an arm to block it and came in under, slashing at Latigo's belly. He heard Latigo grunt. But it did not knock the foreman backward. The man swept Brian's guard aside, laughing hoarsely.

"That high living sure left you like jelly."

The blow came on the last words. It knocked all the wind from Brian. He felt himself stagger backward, a retching sound torn from him. He saw Latigo come into him again and tried to wheel away. He felt Latigo's hands cup over the back of his neck, jerking him down. Then Latigo's knee smashed into his face.

He seemed to spin away in a blinding spasm of pain. He was on the ground. He heard somebody breathing heavily out in front of him and started crawling toward the sound.

"The fool don't know when to quit," somebody in the crowd said. "Kick him again, Latigo. Tear the other ear off —"

The world came down and smashed him on the side of the head and he was spinning again and there was pain and vague sounds all around him and somebody laughing. It took him a long time to realize he was lying on his face against the curb. He tried to lift his head but he couldn't see anything. He made an effort to rise, but could not. He rolled over on his side, pawing blood and dirt from his eyes. Finally dim vision returned. Knots of men were still clustered along the sidewalk, watching him. He recognized Nacho, with an evil leer on his face, and Jigger, still holding a bar towel. Jess Miller had come out of his Mercantile, but made no move to cross the street. Latigo was up on the prancing stallion. From this height he sent one last look down at Sheridan, and spat. Then he raked the Steeldust into a dead run down the street toward his own horse hitched at another rack.

A woman in a blue dress pushed her way through the loose group of men, stepping off the curb. More a girl than a woman. A girl with honey hair swirled around her shoulders by the breeze. He felt a deep humiliation stain his cheeks. Estelle Gillette dropped to her knees beside him, seeking his handkerchief in his coat, dabbing at his face with it.

"I shouldn't feel sorry for you," Estelle said. "But I can't help it." She helped him sit up. "We heard talk. Does this mean it's true?"

He nodded sickly. "I'm wiped out."

"How could they do it? The Double Bit was the biggest thing in this country."

"Tarrant set it up. As long as I was with him, the Salt Rivers couldn't pull his bunch down. But Tarrant must've known the day would come when I'd see how they were using me. I guess he thought I'd knuckle under to save the Double Bit."

"And you didn't?" A strange new light began to shine in her eyes. Then she shook her head in a puzzled way. "But what about George Wolffe? Surely he knew what was going on."

"He tried his best to keep me from living so high. I guess he was really looking out for my best interests. When he saw it was too late I guess he played along with Tarrant to try and pull me out of the hole."

"Where will you go now?"

He shook his head. "I don't know."

"You never took enough of an interest in cattle to know anything about them. You can't keep books. You're too soft for real work."

He stared dully at the street. "I guess you're right. I couldn't get a job any where."

"Especially not in this town. The Salt River bunch hates you too much. The others wouldn't help you for fear of Tarrant. So you'll starve to death. Or join the barflies in the Black Jack. Cadging drinks and scavenging in the garbage pails out back."

He winced under the merciless light of her words. It was an incredible picture she painted, but he realized how close to the truth it was.

"We're staying at Chino Sandoval's," she said. "Why don't you come out there?"

He looked up at her. "That's crazy."

The soft shape of her mouth hardened. "You'd better take the offer. It's the only place you can go."

10

Chino Sandoval had a one-horse outfit up by Mescal Springs, high in the Apaches. It was a land rutted and scarred by the fires of nature till there was little left but bleak buttes and mesa and the eastern backbone of the mountains etching a purple outline against a sun-bleached sky. The springs were but a sink hollowed out of the rocks, dry as bone during the sumnmer days, turned to viscid mud by the water that rose to the surface when night came.

It was a fifteen-mile drive from Apache Wells. Brian was sore and beaten by the ride as well as the fight long before they reached the cut-off that wound up onto the mesa commanding the springs. Here, in the feeble shade of scrawny cottonwoods, were the adobe buildings, the ratty fences of ocotillo corrals. A dozen children scampered out of the compound like scared chickens, hiding behind mud walls and in dark doorways, peering owlishly at the wagon as it pulled up before the house. Then the men began to drift in from the corrals. Pa Gillette and Asa were first in sight, stalking toward the wagon.

Surprised anger dug great hollows in Pa's gaunt cheeks.

"What call you got to bring that snake up here, Estelle?"

"It's the only place he could come," Estelle said defiantly. "They've pulled everything out from under him. The Double Bit's wiped out. We've got to give him a chance, Pa."

"Like the chance he give us?" Pa said. Asa wheeled of toward the house, and Pa glanced after him. "Asa, where you going?"

"To get my gun," Asa said.

"You stay out here," Sandoval called, coming up from behind them. "You promise no trouble there be."

Asa paused, reluctantly, looking back at him. Sandoval was a small wiry man with all fat melted off his bones by the sun and grinding hardships of this arid country. His eyes were a startling blue in an almost negroid face. One of the dozen children peering around the corner of the house had blond hair. It lent a dubious credence to Sandoval's claim that he was pure Yaqui Mayo, descended from the shipwrecked Norsemen who were supposed to have landed at the mouth of the Mayo River hundreds of years before the Spaniards came.

Estelle dropped to the ground, voice intense. "You've got Brian wrong, Pa. He didn't order anybody to foreclose on us. Just a few days after the fight in town he came out to tell us we didn't have to move, and we shot at him."

140

"Shot at him!"

"Maybe you didn't know about it," Brian said, looking at Asa. "It was up at Skeleton Canyon."

"Asa was with me all that day," Pa stormed. "So was Cameron. We was moving down here. Chino can vouch for that."

"*Es verdad,*" the Yaqui said. "It is the truth."

A pair of Mexican hands had moved up behind Sandoval. Cameron Gillette was coming heavily in after them. Sheridan looked around the circle of their hostile faces.

"Somebody bushwacked me in the canyon," he said. "If it hadn't been for that, I'd have been out to tell you to stay on your land."

"It was all some deal of Tarrant's," Estelle said. "He knew the Salt River bunch would be lost without you, Pa. The very fact that they've ruined Brian should be proof enough of where he stands."

The anger still moved turgidly through Pa's face. Asa spat disgustedly and said, "It's some trick. I say fill him full of buckshot if he ain't off here in two minutes."

"Why should man his size stoop to trick?" Sandoval asked. "I knew his father. The Sheridans are no like that."

Estelle turned toward the Yaqui. "You helped us when we needed it, Chino. Now help him. He needs it worse than we do."

From the pouch at his belt, Sandoval pulled a bundle of *hojas.* He fingered one of these pieces of Indian corn husk, tapping into it a small quantity of tobacco from a small tube also contained in the pouch.

"I never thought I see the day a Sheridan to me would come for help," he murmured. He put the *hojas* back into the pouch, rolling the cigarette. "Can cattle you work?"

"He'll learn," Estelle said.

From the pouch, Sandoval now pulled flint and steel and a red cord of tinder. He struck a spark from the flint with the steel *eslabon,* and it lodged in the tinder. He blew it into flame and lit his cigarette.

"At his hands look. Like lilies. Can a man so soft learn about work in one lifetime?"

"Just give him a chance," Estelle said.

"You'll have to work like hell. Everybody out here they have to work like hell. The land she's like that."

"I'll try to pay for my keep, Chino."

Sandoval grinned suddenly. "Then w'at you sit there for?"

Brian got stiffly out of the wagon. Over the sweaty rumps of the team, he saw Pa still staring at him. There was truculent hatred in the man's eyes, and Sheridan realized this was far from settled.

Brian slept that night in a bear-grass hut down by the springs with the Gillettes and the two Mexican hands. He got little sleep, tossing restlessly on the hard corn-shuck pallet, listening to the stertorous snores of the tall, thin hand called

Juan. It was still dark when Sandoval came in and shook him by the shoulder.

"Drag your navel, you lazy *cucurachas*. Is time to roll out if we be at Canyon Moro by sunup."

They rolled out cursing and grumbling. Estelle was with the women up by the house, serving coffee and beef and beans. Still sore and stiff from his beating, Brian almost gagged on the greasy food. With a clatter of tinware the men tossed empty plates and cups into the wreck-pan and drifted toward the corrals. When Brian reached the corral, Pancho came over with a rawhide jumper and a pair of Mexican *chapareros* slung over one arm.

"Here's clothes, *señor*. Better get extra pair of pants from somebody too. Those thorns out on the *malpais* they stab like the dirk. Chino he tell me to help with your horses. That one with the lobo stripe down his back has lots of bottom."

Brian struggled into the jumper and chaps. The man thrust a *maguey* rope into his hands and they moved into the mill of animals lifting a curtain of dust over the corral. Juan and Sandoval and the three Gillettes were all roping their animals out, shouting and cursing. Brian got kicked down trying to dab an awkward loop on the lobo-striped dun. Pancho finally heeled the animal and put a blind on him while he was down. Then he got a Mexican-tree saddle of the top bar of the corral and slung it on. With fumbling hands, Brian cinched it up. He was drenched with sweat and caked with dust by the time he was through. Pancho helped him rope out two more horses for his string. Then Brian stepped aboard his dun. It started pitching before he got his right leg swung over the saddle, and he went off like an empty sack. He heard Cameron laugh derisively from somewhere in the dust. Sandoval came riding up on a nervous buckskin.

"These horse got little more vinegar than ones you're used to, no, *amigo?*"

Brian tried again and this time stayed on. After the bronc got rid of its morning orneriness cat-backing around the corral it settled down. And they rode.

He had no measure of time. Or of the distance they covered. When it was light enough to see, they had reached a spot where a half-dozen brush-filled canyons opened out into a sink with a cow trail leading down every wash to the water. Sandoval said they would round the cattle up while they were drinking and run them down to the flats where they'd have swing room for their ropes.

The men sat sourly in their saddles, half asleep. With the first touch of sun the cattle came, spooky, wild creatures, testing the air with their lifted snouts, shambling down to the water. Brian peered through the milky dawn at their gaunt silhouettes.

"How can you make any money off that beef?" he whispered.

"We don't," Sandoval said. "That's why small

we remain while big you get. Cattle don't put on any lard in the badlands. But jack rabbits they won't take in Alta, *amigo*. We do the best we can."

Juan came threading in through a coulee from the higher land, whispering hoarsely, "That is all, *señores*. We can jump them now."

With a whoop, they rushed down on the herd. The cattle jumped like scared jacks and headed at a dead run down the canyon. His nimble-footed horse took Brian in a wild scrambling run down the steep pitch of the canyon, driving the frenzied cattle into the flats. The Gillettes were waiting by the branding fires and they surrounded the cattle and put them into a mill. While they held them, the cutting and branding began.

"Cut me out that brindle with the gotch horn," Pa shouted.

Brian put his bronc into the herd. A cow took a swipe at him and he almost got gored. He wheeled his bronc and got pinched between two milling heifers. He tore one leg off his chaps getting out of that, and by the time he pulled free the brindle was out of sight.

"Cut me out a dogie, if you can't do any better than that," Pa roared. "That pied one right in front of you."

Brian saw the motherless calf ahead of him and touched his excited horse with a heel. The animal drove in behind the dogie, forcing it out into the open. The little calf tried to wheel back at the fringe of the herd and Brian cut in between it and the other cows, turning it back. The air was so thick with dust he could no longer see Pa, but he pushed the dogie hard toward the spot the man had been in. Too late, he saw the rope ahead of him. It was stretched taut from Asa's buckskin to a downed steer. Asa had dallied his end of the line around the saddle horn and was just swinging off. The dogie bit the stretched rope first, tripping on it and going down. Brian saw Asa's horse jerk. One foot out of the stirrup, Asa threw himself back into the saddle to keep from being pitched. Brian tried to wheel his horse away but he was going too fast. He ran into the line a second after the dogie hit.

This jerked Asa's horse so heavily it almost lost its feet. Dancing to remain erect, it spun around into Brian's animal as he wheeled to the right. He saw the dallied rope pull free and fall to the ground. The steer scrambled erect and disappeared in the dust, line trailing.

Asa's horse tried to dance away from Brian's line-back. Asa reined it back in till he was knee to knee with Brian, grabbing at his jumper.

"Damn you," he shouted. "You did that on purpose."

Brian tried to tear free but Asa hung on. A sudden shift of their excited horses unbalanced Brian and he pitched into Asa, carrying him out of the saddle. They hit heavily. Brian rolled groggily away from Asa. The wiry Gillette gained his feet first and jumped Brian, lashing one boot out to rowel Brian's face with the spur.

There was the smashing detonation of a shot. Brian heard the whining ricochet of metal. He stared wide-eyed at the boot lifted above his face, seeing that the rowel was gone from the spur.

"You better put it down on the ground, Asa," Sandoval said. "Next time your foot I shoot off."

Asa let his boot drop back to the ground beside Brian's face. Brian rolled over onto hands and knees. Sandoval was sitting a dancing horse right above them, a smoking Colt in his hand.

"Now back to work get, both of you," he said. "Any more of this and the welcome of my house she's no longer yours."

For two weeks the roundup continued. Days that never seemed to end. Up before dawn and in the saddle till long after dark. Sleeping in stupefied exhaustion through a night too short to give a man any real rest. The wink of branding fires in the velvet dark. The constant stench of sweat and burning hair and hot dust. Brian lost weight till his clothes hung on him and his face was raw from the burn of sun and wind and his whole body ached with the slightest movement.

A hundred times he was ready to quit. It was hard to say why he stayed. Sometimes it was Asa's goading, making him stick in sheer bitter defiance. Sometimes it was the shy friendship of Sandoval, filling him with a warmth he had never felt with Jess Miller or the other men he had thought were close to him. Sometimes it was

147

his own stubbornness, a stubbornness he had never known he possessed before, lengthening that long upper lip into a fighting shape and putting him back into the nightmare.

After the branding was over they cut out the young stuff and started the beef toward Alta. They had long since used up the coffee and beans Estelle had gotten at Apache Wells, and were living exclusively on their own beef. But they had no time to stop off at the ranch. Sandoval had started roundup early in the hopes of beating the big operators into Alta, and it would be touch and go from now on.

They drove west out of the Apaches and into the alkali furnace of the flats southeast of the Superstitions. At this time of year there was so little water that they worked on a dangerously close margin between sinks. They reached Denver Wells and found it dry. They pushed a herd frantic with thirst on toward Rabbit Sink, the next waterhole, the men as hollow-eyed and driven as the animals.

They topped a sandhill east of the sink near nightfall, and saw that the cattle had run up against something ahead. In the haze of wind-blown sand, all Brian could see was the dim forms of the beasts milling back and forth in the flats, as if held by an invisible wall. Sandoval and Brian put their jaded horses to a trot, rounding the herd and catching sight of Asa and Pa Gillette ahead. Then Brian saw the triple strand of barb-wire.

"This sink belongs to Sid Bouley, doesn't it?" Asa said acidly. "I thought he was still with the Salt River bunch."

Cameron looked at his brother, then shook his head. "Bouley was always a weak bet, Asa. Looks like he went over to Tarrant when he heard Pa was squeezed out."

"We'll cut the wire, damn it," Pa said. "Juan, bring up that hatchet. These cattle will die if they don't get this water."

The thin Mexican galloped up, pulling a hatchet from his bedroll. The cattle were frenzied with their thirst, milling against the fence in a bawling press. Sandoval told Asa to hold the beef there till he found out if there was any water. Brian and Pa went with him through the hole Juan chopped. Three hundred yards on they came to the sloping banks of the sink. In the dusk, Sandoval was a vague shadow, dismounting.

"Is mud. The water in an hour should surface," he turned to call. "Start them through."

It was getting so dark Brian could not see the cattle at first. He knew they were beginning to move, for their bawling grew to a raucous crescendo. Then the ground began to tremble and the first tossing heads appeared out of the gloom. Sandoval toed his stirrup and started to swing up.

Then the gunshot came, like the crack of a giant whip. Brian's startled horse screamed in fright and reared high. He put a rein against its neck and spurred a sweaty flank, bringing the animal back down and spinning it to keep the beast from bolting. More shots formed a crackling drumbeat in the night. Brian fought his spinning horse, staring into the darkness in a vain attempt to see where the shots came from. Sandoval's horse had bolted while he was still only half on and he was racing away from the sink, striving to gain the saddle.

"It's coming from those north ridges," Pa shouted. "The cattle are stampeding —"

His voice broke off sharply, amid the drumming bursts of gunfire, and Brian saw him pitch from his saddle. The ground was shaking with the rush of cattle now and Brian knew he had but a moment to reach the man. He spurred the frightened line-back across the sandy flats, pulling it down hard where Pa's gaunt form stirred feebly on the ground.

"Grab a stirrup, Pa," he shouted. "I'll have to drag you out."

The man made a feeble attempt to lift his arm, dropped back. Brian swung down and tried to hold his frenzied horse and catch Pa under the armpits. As he heaved the man up, meaning to throw him over the saddle, more shots split the night. The line-back reared, snapping the reins from Brian's hand, and bolted. He was left holding Pa halfway off the ground, without a horse.

The tossing heads and curving horns of the cattle seemed to be right on top of them. Brian had a dim glimpse of a rider off to one side, and heard Juan's high voice: "Run to the left, Brian. I can't turn them! You can make it to the left!"

Brian let Pa's limp weight slide to the ground, his whole body jerked with the impulse to wheel and race for safety. But something held him. A thought from long ago was in his mind. And Jigger's words: "It can't be done. It's just one of those stories you hear about Tiger Sheridan." Even as it ran through him, Brian was reaching for the match in a hip pocket and wiping it against his Levis. It didn't catch. The ground was quaking beneath him and it seemed another instant would bring the whole herd down on him. He struck the match again.

It flared, wavered. He cupped it in his hand. He held it that way, standing spraddle-legged over Pa Gillette's body. His whole being was torn by the impulse to escape the destruction of those tossing horns and cloven hoofs bearing down on him.

For that last moment he stared up at the oncoming phalanxes, and thought he was through. Jigger was right. It couldn't be done.

Then the steer right before him reared into the air, eyes rolling wildly in animal fear of fire. The next animal veered the other way, bawling in senseless fright at that small, winking flame. The others followed suit blindly, splitting around Brian. He was an island in a sea of sweaty bodies and tossing horns. The light flickered, seemed to die. He saw a heifer racing right at him. Desper-

151

ately he cupped his hands about the match. The flame flared again. The heifer threw her head back to bawl and almost lost her feet turning aside in the last instant.

If it had been a Double Bit gather, he would never have lasted it out. But the very meagerness of Sandoval's outfit saved him. It seemed an eternity. It seemed a second. Finally they were gone, leaving him standing above Pa, unable to tell whether the earth was still trembling beneath him, or whether he was shaking in reaction. The match burned his fingers and he threw it from him. Its light winked out and left the blackness of night.

11

It was near evening of the next day that they got back to Sandoval's ranch. Asa and Cameron rode with Pa between them and Brian brought up the rear. They couldn't have gotten a wagon out to the Rabbit Sink Country, so they had been forced to bring Pa back on his horse. It had been a cruel ride for him, and he was half-delirious in the saddle.

Estelle was the first to come from the house, staring blankly at the little group of alkali-covered riders, then breaking forward with a sharp cry. Brian dismounted and helped Cameron ease the elder Gillette out of his saddle. Pa opened fever-rimmed eyes as Estelle reached him, suppressed hysteria in her pale face.

"It's all right, daughter," he said feebly. "Little gunshot wound ain't going to hurt me after what we went through. Brian saved my life. He's a real Sheridan all right. Nobody'd ever believe that story about his pa. He proved it. Just a match like that. Just a little match —"

He winced and sagged forward against Sheridan. With a small sob, Estelle turned and helped them half carry him toward the house. It was then that Brian noticed the two dusty horses at the door, and the pair of men who had followed Estelle.

Morton Forge was a thick-muscled man in a linsey-woolsey coat and brush-scarred leggings of rawhide, the ruddy hue of a perpetually sun-burned face glowing faintly through a gray mask of alkali. Ring Partridge was smaller, his narrow shoulders stooped in their horsehide vest, his sun-squinted eyes smoldering with an old hatred. Last year Wolffe had foreclosed on the long-overdue notes of both these men. Seeing the unveiled hostility in their faces, Brian knew an impulse to try and explain how little contact he'd had with the business of the Double Bit. Then he shrugged it away, knowing how useless apology was now.

"I never thought I'd see you riding with Salt River," Partridge said acidly.

Forge put a rope-gnarled hand on Partridge's arm. "Never mind, Ring. What happened out there, Brian?"

"Somebody's put bobwire around Rabbit Sink," Brian said. "When we tried to drive the beef through, they started shooting. The cattle scattered out into the badlands north of the sink. Sandoval's out there trying to round them up."

"What now?" Partridge asked.

"I'm riding for the doctor."

"Doc Manning is Tarrant's cousin."

154

"What's the difference? He'll come."

"Sure he will," Forge said. "He's decent enough. But that won't keep him from talking. It'll bust the Salt Rivers for good if it gets around that Pa Gillette's wounded this bad. Pa was all that held us together."

"It was bad enough when you foreclosed on him," Partridge said. "A lot of borderline men thought we were finished. They hopped right over to Tarrant."

Forge nodded. "Tarrant's working like hell to get enough signatures on that recall petition. But he hasn't got fifty-one per cent yet. If we can only hang on till Mayor Prince gets the franchise voted through, we'll be safe." Brian saw the wisdom in their talk. If it got out that Pa was hit this bad, men like Sid Bouley and Wirt Peters would go over to Tarrant immediately. Maybe Bouley had already gone over, by the looks of the wire around Rabbit Sink.

Asa came to the door. The boy's eyes were like holes burned through the dust-caked mask of his gaunt face.

"Sandoval's wife got the bullet out," he said.

"How's the wound?" Brian asked.

"Little swollen. The Indian woman says she can draw it out with a poultice. I think Pa's main trouble is loss of blood. He wants to see you."

Brian and the other two entered the squalid mud *jacal.* A pot-fire flickered in one corner, a stew kettle hanging over it. Stooped over the kettle was Quita, Sandoval's tubby Indian wife, stirring a stinking mess of piñon gum and creosote leaves that was to be the poultice for the wound. Pa Gillette lay on a pallet next to the wall, Estelle on her knees beside him.

"I heard what you said outside," Pa told them feebly. "Don't ride for the doctor."

Brian shook his head. "I don't feel right about it."

"You don't know these Yaquis," Pa said. "I've seen Quita heal men Doc Manning gave up for dead."

For some reason Brian looked at Estelle. She met his eyes soberly, nodding. "I trust her, Brian."

It decided him. "All right. Just promise me one thing. If Pa gets worse you'll send for the doctor."

They all nodded in silent agreement. Brian turned and went outside. Now that it was over, reaction began to set in. His exhaustion struck him like a blow and he felt sick and began to tremble. Forge and Partridge followed him out.

"I'll be going back to help Sandoval with those cattle," Brian said. "Why don't you come along?"

"With you?" Partridge's voice was sarcastic.

"It's not for me," Brian said angrily. "It's for Sandoval."

"We ain't got any beef in the herd," Partridge said.

"You're still with the Salt Rivers, aren't you?"

"Yeah."

"Then do it for them. If Tarrant stops Sandoval from this drive you might as well give up."

Forge frowned at the smaller man, scratching thoughtfully at his ruddy face. "Boy's right, Ring," Forge said. "Sandoval's about our last hope."

Brian heard a stir in the doorway and turned to see that Estelle had been standing there, a cup in her hand. "You can't go now," she said. "You'd pass out."

He smiled wearily. "You're right. How about first thing in the morning?"

Forge nodded. Partridge did not react. He stared at Brian a moment, the suspicion deepening weather-tracks around his narrow eyes. Then both he and Forge turned and headed for their horses, hitched at the corral. Silently Brian watched till the men reached the animals. They stood by the horses a moment, talking; then they began to unsaddle. Brian turned to see Estelle smiling at him. He returned the smile and she held the cup of steaming coffee out.

"Quita's getting up a plate of food, too," she said. She was silent, watching as he drank. Then she said, "Brian . . . how can I thank you?"

He looked at her, remembering when their whole relationship had been a gay, bantering duel. He had never been able to penetrate her defenses, verbally or otherwise. But now a change had come. Her face held a different expression from any he'd ever seen before; it was soft, accepting. There were no defenses to penetrate. A short time ago he would have pressed his advantage.

He handed the cup back. "One of those things, Estelle. Pa would have done the same thing for me."

Her breathing lifted her breasts. They formed a round, high shape against the dress. It made him suddenly conscious of her whole body. Summer corn and fresh-baked bread and a sweet spring wind. The blood thickened in his throat.

She saw the change in his face and moistened her lips. "Brian —"

He waited expectantly. She did not continue. Her body seemed to settle, to move away from him. Her cheeks were flushed and her tawny eyes had grown veiled.

"What is it?" he asked.

"Nothing." She put her hands together and looked down at them. "If you're going in the morning you'd better get some rest."

"Yeah. I guess I had."

She raised her eyes to him for a last time. Then she turned and went into the house. He waited a moment, finally began walking toward the beargrass huts down by the river. He had gone all the way before he remembered that Estelle had said Quita was getting a plate of food for him. He stopped by the door, eyes closed with exhaustion. Morton Forge came from inside.

"We stowed our gear in there for tonight," he said. "You going to eat?"

Brian shook his head dully. "Tell Quita I'm too tired. You take my plate."

Forge nodded. Partridge joined him and they went toward the main house. Brian stumbled inside. Estelle was still in his mind. He wanted to think about something. He was too tired. He knew he could think about it if he wasn't so tired, It was about Estelle. Something about Estelle. He rolled into a bunk without even bothering to undress. He went to sleep before he thought to pull a cover up.

They rose next morning just after dawn. Quita was already up, making their coffee, heating their tortillas and beans. They ate hurriedly, shivering and groggy in the early chill. Then they rode — Brian and Partridge and Forge and the two Gillette brothers.

It was a grueling ride, through the hottest part of the day. Sandoval had set up a half-faced camp on the rim of the badlands a few miles north of Rabbit Sink. The men reached it near evening, faces alkali-whitened masks, clothes turned to a clammy paste by sweat and dust. There was an ocotillo corral jammed into a box-end gully, holding a pitiful handful of the Yaqui's cattle. Pancho stood guard on the ridge, a sleepy, cat-nervous sentry with an old Sharp's buffalo gun loaded and cocked in the crook of one arm. He told them Sandoval was still back in the badlands gathering the stampeded cattle. Quita had sent coffee with them and they made a pot and sat around the juniper fire drinking it, bitter and black, while the sun went down. In the following darkness Sandoval and Juan returned with a dozen more mangy head of beef. They drove the cattle into the corral and then swung off their briny horses. Exhaustion and defeat seemed to deepen the gaunt hollows in the Yaqui's primitive face.

"At this rate it take us all year to get in those cattle," he said.

"We got two fresh hands to help," Brian told him.

The Indian glanced at Forge and Partridge without hope. "So we get the beef. So what then?"

"We go on to Alta," Brian said.

"Without water?"

"We can find a new route. There are other sinks."

"Fenced in too."

Brian frowned at him. "How can you be so sure?"

Sandoval sat down on a saddle, pulling a *hoja* from the pouch at his belt, building a cigarette. "You think Bouley put this wire up?"

"He owns Rabbit Sink."

"Juan he tell me funny thing. Some of the men who shoot at us they also ride in to stampede cattle. Juan he get a good look at one. Latigo. Riding your Steeldust."

Brian could not answer for a moment. He knew it should hold no shock for him, no surprise. Latigo was still handling the Double Bit cattle. Though he was technically now working for the court, his allegiance still remained to the ranch. And that ranch had been allied with Tarrant and all his interests for years.

"You think Tarrant did this?" Partridge said angrily.

Sandoval nodded. He dragged deep on his smoke. "The last of the Salt Rivers I am with any big herd. What you think it do to us if I no get through to Alta this year?"

Partridge began to pace around the fire, a stringy, bowlegged man, too exasperated to remain still. "I bet they got every free sink between here and Alta strung up with wire."

"Or poisoned, or guarded," Forge said. "What's the difference? I think Sandoval's right. This is Tarrant's big bid to stop us for good."

"We could fight 'em," Asa said hotly.

They looked at him without answering. They all knew that Tarrant had the combined crews of half a dozen of the biggest ranches in the state at his bidding. They would outnumber the Salt Rivers ten to one. It would be a stupid gesture to throw Sandoval's pitiful group against such a force. The first clash would cut them to pieces, would leave them without enough men to handle the herd. Asa cursed softly and turned away, kicking spitefully at the gear on the ground.

Through the past moments, as their true position had become clear to Brian, something had been turning over in his mind. It was a gamble.

But when a man's back was to the wall, what did he have left?

"How about going in the back door to Alta?" he asked.

They all stared at him. In the flickering firelight their faces were drawn and chalky masks. Finally Forge said, "You mean up over the Rim?"

Brian nodded. "Circle north. Through the reservation if we have to. Down into the Tonto."

He stopped. He hadn't meant to stop. Hadn't wanted to. But they all knew what was next and the expression on their faces stopped him and before he could continue again Partridge finished it for him.

"Dammit," Partridge said, "who's going through the Superstitions?"

"It'd be suicide!"

"How could we do it?"

"Tarrant would be on us before we topped the Rim —"

It came at Brian from all sides. He shouted to be heard over their voices. "You forget Tarrant's got his men down here. If we move at all, they expect us to take the old route. They'll be watching those sinks like hawks. The last thing in the world they'll look for is a drive through their own back yard. If they do find out they'll be a hundred miles behind us. There's plenty of water up on the Rim. We can drive at night and cover ourselves."

"So Tarrant doesn't find us," Asa said. "We

still come up against the same thing at the end."

"Damn right," Partridge said. "My brother disappeared in them Superstitions fifteen years ago. I ain't taking no cattle through there."

It was Brian's turn for anger. "Then where in hell are you taking 'em?"

None of them answered. They scowled at each other, fingered their faces, toed the dirt. Finally Sandoval flipped his smoke into the darkness and rose.

"Is my cattle we talk about," he said. He looked northwest into the night, toward the Superstitions. "Maybe Brian he is right. Maybe that is the only way left."

A haunted look came to Juan's seamed face. He crossed himself and shook his head. "I ride for you fifteen years, Chino, but I no can go there for you."

Pancho moved closer to Sandoval. "I can."

Sandoval smiled and put his arm across Pancho's shoulder. He looked questioningly at Brian.

"It was my idea, wasn't it?" Brian asked.

"And you're stuck with it," Partridge said.

"I'll go," Forge said quietly.

"Thanks, Morton," Brian said. He was looking at Asa. The youngest Gillette met his gaze with smoldering eyes. Brian knew that Asa was still deeply suspicious of him, hostile despite what Brian had done for Pa. And Brian knew that Cameron would follow whatever decision Asa made.

Brian had the impulse to remind Asa how Sandoval had taken them in when no one else would defend them. But Asa was a hotheaded young fool without much room for moral obligation in his life. Brian figured that the only thing he could appeal to was the boy's inflated ego.

"Maybe you haven't got the guts," he said.

A rush of blood darkened Asa's face. He spat disgustedly. "I'll last as long as you," he said.

Partridge began moving again, scowling and kicking at the gear. "I'll stand up to a fair fight, anybody knows that. You know that, Mort. I'll stand up to a fair fight —"

"Forget it," Brian told him. "You've made your choice. Just do one thing for us." Partridge stopped fidgeting and frowned at Brian. "When you get back to Apache Wells," Brian said, "spread the word that it'll take us a couple of weeks to round up these cattle. And that we're still going to try and drive across the desert."

Partridge shook his head. "You're a bunch of damn fools," he said. He looked of toward the Superstitions. "You're all just a bunch of damn fools."

12

After Ring Partridge and Juan left camp, Brian told the others what was on his mind. There was little doubt that Tarrant had men watching them. Sandoval had seen riders that morning and Pancho had found shod tracks at some distance more than once. However, as long as cattle remained in the pen with a guard over them, it was logical to assume the Tarrant men would think that this was home base and that Sandoval was still trying to round up his cattle in the badlands.

"So we'll leave some cattle here," Brian said.

"I can't afford to sacrifice any beef," Sandoval said.

"What about those sick ones in the pen?" Brian asked. They all looked at the corral. The cruel heat and lack of water had taken its toll. A dozen of the steers in the pen were either dying or too sick to make the next warerhole. "And there must be others out in the badlands," Brian said. "Those are the ones we'll leave."

They rose before dawn the next morning and started out to the gather. It was an even more grueling process than the first roundup. It was a forgotten land, more twisted, more burned than that around Mescal Springs. The diamond-glitter of exposed rock faces blinded them half the time; the sun fried their brains and the heat simmered in maddening waves on every horizon. They had to dismount every few minutes to clean out the clogged nostrils of their animals. It was a titanic battle to catch every steer they sighted. The cattle were crazed with thirst and ran like mad things before the riders.

It was no weather to run a horse in and they killed two before noon. Forge got so sick he had to go back to camp and Cameron Gillette passed out while he was roping down a steer. But somehow they kept at it, half-blind, really from the heat, growing as frantic as the animals with thirst.

They gathered half a hundred steers before dark and held them in a box canyon with a pair of *maguey* ropes stretched across its mouth. A dozen of the steers were obviously too far gone to drive. These Brian and Sandoval took back to the corral, riding ridges and open country so the Tarrant men would be sure to spot them. Under cover of darkness they then returned to the badlands.

It was Sandoval's Indian knowledge of the country that saved them and kept them going. Like some animal, he was able to locate where the water rose to the surface after the sun was gone. He spent half the night circling camp and locating these seeps. The water was half mud and each seep contained enough for only a few men or animals, but it sustained them for the next day's hellish struggle.

Forge finally got so sick they had to stretch him out under a cover made from his two saddle blankets. He spent the night in delirium and was too feeble to ride the following day.

But it looked as though their ruse was working. They kept trailing the sick cattle to the corral every evening. The Tarrant men, apparently assuming that this was all they could catch, were certainly not going to ride into the living hell of the badlands just to watch a roundup.

And finally the nightmare ended. They had regained the bulk of their herd and were ready to drive again. Though still too sick to ride with them, Forge said he would stay at the corral and perpetuate their ruse. Every night he would drive a dozen sick cattle into the badlands under the cover of darkness. He would hold them there till the next day and then drive them back to the pen. The Tarrant men had not yet shown themselves very close, and such activity might deceive a distant watcher long enough to give the main herd a head start.

The animals were in such bad condition now that they had to reach the water on the Rim as soon as possible. It meant taking a chance and using the quickest route, the Salt River Trail. They sent Pancho to scout the way and headed northeast through the badlands. Driving at night, bedding down during the day, they sighted the trail on the second dawn. They bedded down a mile west, in a canyon where Sandoval had found a seep. Pancho rode into camp just as the sun seemed to explode from the edge of the world. He had sighted a pair of riders in the predawn darkness, coming toward the herd.

Sandoval and Brian rode back with the Mexican. They topped a ridge where ocotillo bloom flamed like burning candles and lonely saguaros pointed their sentinel fingers at a steel-bright sky. Below them a pair of riders were already toiling up the rugged slope toward them, half-hidden in a haze of dust. Pancho started pulling his saddlegun from its scabbard. Brian stopped him.

"You should have waited till daylight," he said. "That's Wirt Peters's claybank."

Sandoval let out a relieved sigh. They held their horses till Wirt Peters reached them. With him was one of his Mexican hands, Iguala, broad, paunchy, fifty, with a grizzled mat of gray hair and a sloping Aztec brow. Peters's beefy face was running with sweat and his eyes were blank with surprise.

"What the hell are you doing here?"

Brian grinned humorlessly. "We might ask the same."

"Trailing strays. They always head for this seep." Peters cuffed his hat back, looking at the herd in the canyon. He began to scratch at his blond beard stubble. He alway did that when he was puzzled. "Ring Partridge said you was following the desert route to Alta."

"That's what we wanted him to say."

Peters looked from Brian to Sandoval. "You ain't goin' up over the Rim?"

"That's right."

"You'll have to go through the Superstitions."

"That's right."

Iguala emitted a moan and crossed himself.

"Why don't you throw in?" Sandoval asked.

Peters shifted his heavy frame in the saddle. He scowled at the ground. "Hell," he said.

"You don't get some beef to Alta this year you might as well quit."

Peters scratched his jaw again. "Saw Tarrant in town yesterday. He said if I wanted to wait till fall I could use their water along the desert route."

"All you had to do was sign the petition," Brian said.

Peters flushed. "I didn't sign nothing."

"Then what the hell are you talking about?" Brian said.

Peters shook his head again, frowning at the ground. "The Superstitions," he said.

"You hear what happen at Rabbit Sink," Sandoval said. "How else would you do it?"

Peters scratched savagely at his jaw. "Damm it," he said. Then he looked angrily at Iguala. The man made a bleating sound and shook his head back and forth.

"No, *señor*, not the Superstitions, not Iguala —"

"How about the edge of the Tonto?" Brian asked.

The Mexican considered it a moment. Then he nodded dubiously. "Maybe I go that far." He crossed himself again. "No farther."

Peters looked at Brian and sighed heavily. "I guess I'm just dumb. I'll throw in with you."

They could not wait for Peters. It would take him a couple of days to get underway but his herd was fresh and he could push harder. He said he'd meet them at Three Crossings in the reservation. That evening they pushed on north along the Salt River Trail. It took them uncomfortably close to Apache Wells but they planned to pass it and be in the broken land along the edge of the Rim before dawn.

It was night when they reached the road leading into town. They chose a much-used cattle crossing so their tracks would be hidden in the others. When the herd was on the other side Sandoval rode up to Brian, leading his black roping horse.

"Everybody they think we take the desert route. To be seen in town it would hurt us?"

"Maybe we could risk it. Why?"

"No more grub. We can't get it all out of the country."

"None of us has a cent. Who'd give us credit?"

The Yaqui looked at his black roper. "Maybe a way I got."

They told Asa to keep the herd moving. It was about ten miles to town. They knew that Jess Miller stayed open till nine on Friday. They had to push hard to make it. There was little traffic abroad. The crews of the big outfits were still occupied with the tail end of calf roundup or were detailed to watch the desert route they thought Sandoval was taking with his herd. Cochise Street itself was all but deserted. The only life it showed came in the yellow channels of light thrown from the windows of the store, the occasional bursts of sound coming from the Black Jack. As Brian and Sandoval racked their horses before the Mercantile, Brian could not help the glance he sent across the street toward the feed store. The windows on its second floor were alight, silhouetting the peeling gilt letters on an upper pane: *George Wolffe, Attorney at Law*.

Brian trailed Sandoval into the store. Jess Miller was helping a pair of bonneted women near the rear. When he saw the two men he gaped in surprise, then came hesitantly forward. He passed beneath an overhead lamp. The shadows it cast made his face look froglike.

"Brian," he said. His eyes blinked, trying to meet Brian's gaze squarely. He seemed acutely embarrassed, at a loss for words. Finally he looked at Sandoval. "I thought you were driving south?"

The Yaqui grinned. "Some grub we need."

"I can't extend you any more credit, Chino —"

"Not on cows that ain't going to make it to Alta, is that it?"

"I — I —"

"Negrito he is outside."

Miller's fat mouth closed. He looked past Sandoval and a covetous light came to his eyes. He moistened his lips. Sandoval wheeled and tramped out again, his spurs setting up a big clatter in the room. Miller followed. Brian saw that the women had pulled back against the wall, watching him like a pair of frightened hens. For some strange reason it made him feel good. He grinned derisively at them and trailed the other two men out. Miller was standing on the curb, thumbs hooked in the armholes of his bed-of-flowers waistcoat, lips pursed, rocking back and forth on his heels studying the black roper in the feeble light that came from the door.

"Ain't in such good condition, Chino."

"I been work him. A month in pasture, as good as new he'll be."

"Sounds like he's sucking a little wind."

"The price you can't knock down. I know how much you always want him, Jess. A hundred dollars you offer last time."

"Give you fifty — in grub."

"Seventy-five."

"Sixty."

"Sold."

Miller sent the Yaqui a birdlike glance. Then he turned so Sandoval would not see his triumphant smirk. He passed Brian, going back inside. Sandoval stepped of the curb and stood close to the black. He put his palm against the horse's neck. He wasn't looking at the horse or anything else. Finally he cleared his throat and came back on the sidewalk. He wouldn't meet Brian's eyes as he passed.

"Keep watch," he said. "I get the grub."

Brian stood in the light a moment, heedless of it. He looked at the black. He knew what the horse meant to Sandoval. It made him feel like hell.

Before he moved out of the light he saw George Wolffe's door open. Someone stepped onto the landing and light burned for that moment against a woman's shape. She stopped on the landing, staring across the street toward the Mercantile, and he knew she had seen him in the light.

Arleen.

She came down the stairs and across the Street. Expectancy was like a cotton gag in his throat. How could she always do that to him? Just the glimpse of her at a distance.

Light from the Mercantile's open door sent its soft glow into the street and picked up her form. She wore a dress of flowered chintz, its full skirt switching back and forth with the free movement of her hips. She was hatless and her face was a pale oval against the black mass of lustrous hair. She held a reticule in one hand and he knew she had meant to come across for some shopping. Probably a pound of coffee, he thought wryly. They always seemed to run out when George had night work. It was odd to remember these little things about them. It seemed so long ago that they had formed a part of his life.

She stepped up onto the walk and stopped. The light shone softly against the high peaks of her exotic cheekbones and made little pinpoints of glitter in her black eyes. She seemed to search for something in his face. Finally she said, softly, "Brian."

"Arleen."

She hesitated. Then, stiffly: "I thought you were with Sandoval."

"We had to come in for some grub."

He rebelled against the absurdity of the prosaic. There was so much else to be said. Yet he felt blocked, held back. Her nearness brought the old excitement. The soft white throat, the shape of her breasts, the supple hips beneath the skirt. The cotton seemed to thicken in his throat. His face felt hot and he was angry with himself that this had not changed. Because too many other things had changed. It was not the same. Too many new barriers stood between them.

She took a step closer. "Are you really going to try a desert drive?"

"Ring Partridge must have been in town," he said.

"Surely you know what you're getting into."

"Are you warning me?"

She made a hopeless little sound. "Why didn't you give in to Tarrant in the beginning? Everything would have been so right."

"Was Tarrant right?"

"For you he was. You belong with the big ones, Brian."

"The ones who helped me when I was down?"

Her body seemed to stiffen. She was searching his face again, both hands gripping the reticule tightly.

"We're talking about the wrong thing," he said. "Why are we afraid to talk about us?"

Some of the tension left Arleen. Her voice had a slack and husky sound. "You wanted me to marry you. Are you asking for the answer now?"

"How could I?" he said. "Sandoval lives in a two-room house with a mud floor. Is that what you want?"

"Don't talk that way. You'll pull out — you'll come back."

"And you'll wait?"

She hesitated. "Is that what *you* want?"

"That's what I'm getting at, Arleen. How can I ask anything of you? You didn't agree to anything. I can't hold you to something that isn't there."

"Maybe you want out. Is that what you're trying to say?"

He was surprised that it should put him on the defensive. "Of course not. I'm just trying to square us away."

"Maybe you're trying too soon, Brian." Her

voice grew husky. "This thing has changed both our lives. We've got to face it. But underneath we're the same. Maybe it will just take time."

He wanted to believe her, wanted to think she was saying she'd wait. Yet somehow he was not convinced. There was an undercurrent of something else, a subtle taint that held him back. He didn't know whether it was in him or in her. Suddenly, with her nearness goading him on, he had the urgent need to take her in his arms, to sweep all the barriers away with the passion they had known before. It was an urge too strong and too elemental to check and he was about to reach for her when the heavy stamp of boots in the doorway halted him.

Sandoval came out carrying a fifty-pound sack of flour on his back and Jess Miller's clerk followed laden with a side of bacon and towsacks of beans and coffee. Sandoval halted, looking embarrassed. Then he touched his hat and murmured a greeting in Spanish and circled around Arleen. The clerk followed. Arleen and Brian stared helplessly at each other. He felt an intense frustration. She moistened her lips. Her voice sounded stiff, brittle.

"Good luck, Brian."

She turned and walked into the store, fumbling in her reticule. The clerk had tied the sacks of coffee and beans behind Brian's saddle. Brian saw Jess Miller approach Arleen inside, bowing and smirking and rubbing his hands like a sycophant. The clerk unhitched the black roper and led him around to the barn behind the store. With a soft and helpless curse Brian wheeled and tramped off the walk and climbed onto his horse. Sandoval finished lashing the flour behind the cantle and mounted up. Near the edge of town they passed a rider coming in. He passed ten feet on their flank, looking at them without speaking or acknowledging them in any way. It was Nacho.

A hundred yards farther on they reached the Mescal Springs Trail. Without even looking at each other they turned onto it. They knew that within half an hour the whole town would think they had turned south into the desert.

"On high ground we'll be in twenty minutes," Sandoval said. "If anybody follow us we see them."

Brian only half heard him. He was looking back at the winking lights of the town. Sandoval knew what was on his mind.

"Well," Sandoval said. "We both leave something behind."

"Yeah," Brian said. "I guess we did."

13

They saw no one following and they caught up with the herd near midnight. They pushed hard and got the cattle up into the rugged tumbling country that formed the climb to the Rim. They bedded down at dawn in a lost canyon where a spring ran with more water than they'd seen in a month. They traded off on watches, two men sleeping, one holding the herd, and two others scouting the surrounding country for any stray riders that might come too close.

It went off without a bobble and that night they got up onto the plateau. They were in different country now. They were on top of the Rim, a mile above the desert. There was water in the creeks and the sage was green on the slopes and the air was like syrup when the wind came from the northeast with its scent of distant pine forests. Wirt Peters caught up with them at Three Crossings, pushing two hundred head of tired and dusty steers. Iguala was with him but his other Mexican hand had refused to come. From Three Crossings they drove directly into the reservation.

On the first morning after crossing the line they bedded down in a tortuous pass south of the Salt River Gorge. Sandoval sent Asa to cover their back trail and Cameron to scout ahead. Brian had taken the scout the previous day, had only known four hours' sleep in the last forty-eight, and was drugged with exhaustion. He stripped his horse and opened out his bedroll while Pancho threw their grub together. The smell of pan bread and boiling Triple X was torture to Brian. He was so exhausted he didn't think he could stay awake long enough to eat.

Sandoval was bringing more wood for the fire. He stopped sharply at the outskirts of camp, hugging the armful of dead wood to his chest and staring eastward.

"They seen us," he said.

Brian turned to look. There was sand in his eyes. He rubbed them, squinting, trying to bring the horizon into focus. Dawn lay in a pearly sheet above the broken rim of country ahead. Then he saw the smoke. It struck at the sky in short puffs at first. Then a long pennant drifted up.

"What're they saying?" Brian asked.

"How many men we got. How many cattle. Which way we go."

"Think they'll bother us?"

"They don't like it."

"How about Tarrant?" Peters asked.

"Too far west he is to see it," Yaqui said.

"Wouldn't do him any good if he did," Brian said. "I don't think there's a man on his crew can read it. Tiger was the only one that paid any heed to these smoke signals."

Peters scrubbed a thumb through his blond beard. "Well — you can't tell about these Apaches."

None of them answered. Finally Sandoval walked to the fire and dropped his wood beside it. Pancho slid the pan off the fire and began to slice the bread. Brian got his utensils from his saddle roll; he filled his tin plate and cup and sat on his saddle to eat. He fell asleep twice before he finished. Then he scoured the cup and plate with sand, tossed it with his other gear, rolled into his blanket fully dressed, and was instantly asleep for the third time. . . .

The smoke signals followed them all the way through the reservation. They never saw the Indians but they knew they were being watched every minute of the time. It was a growing pressure against them, only adding to the tension and exhaustion of the drive itself that had worn the men down till they were nervous and jumpy as cats. Shorthanded, forced to take extra watches, losing their sleep to the constant necessity of scouting, they were all closer to the breaking point than they realized.

But there was still no sign of any Tarrant men when they crossed out of the reservation at Feather Mountain. They pushed west till the Sierra Anchas rose on their flank — somber tumbled peaks mantled with the silvery shimmer of a thousand aspens. At the end of a night's drive they found themselves in a broad basin deep in pine grass and wild clover. It was ideal graze for the tired cattle but too exposed for Brian's peace of mind. Before he would let the herd halt he scouted northwest and ran into the toes of another mountain chain. He returned to find the herd halted and the men gathered at its head.

"There's a lot of spur canyons about a mile up there," he said. "We can cut 'em up in little bunches with a man to each one."

Asa showed temper. "I ain't driving a mile out of the way to sit up all night with a cut of spooky beef."

"We can find box canyons and sleep at the mouth."

"And get clobbered when the beef stampedes over you," Asa said.

"This is the closest we'll be to Tarrant's range," Brian said. "We can't leave them out here in the open."

"Tarrant, hell. If he was gonna jump us he'd of done it before now. You've kept us in the saddle every night with that kind of talk. I ain't going to kill myself just so's you can play the big ramrod."

Sandoval rubbed scarred knuckles against his red-rimmed eyes, speaking wearily. "Brian he's been right up to now. The cattle I think we better put in them spur canyon."

"Go ahead," Asa said. He swung of his horse and began to unlace his bedroll from behind the cantle. "I'm camping right here."

This undercurrent of conflict had run between Asa and Brian from the very beginning and Brian had known that sooner or later it would come to a head. But he was so tired he couldn't even feel angry at the man. He was miserable and drugged with exhaustion and for a moment he didn't give a damn whether Asa camped here or whether Tarrant found them in the next minute or whether the cattle ran off the Rim and broke every one of their fool necks. He wiped a dirty hand across his chapped lips and tried to arouse himself from the lethargy. He heeled his horse over beside Asa and then swung off with a tired wheeze.

Slowly Asa came around to face him. Brian stood slack and wide-legged and sway-backed. His broad shoulders were bowed and in the wan light of dawn his face was a waxen mask of grime and sweat and exhaustion.

"One man camped here in the open would give the whole thing away," he said. "You're going with the rest."

"I ain't going."

"I haven't got much juice left in me, Asa. I'm not going to waste it fighting you."

A contemptuous shape came to Asa's thin lips. "I *thought* it was all hot air."

Brian kicked him in the shin. Asa doubled forward with a sharp cry of pain. Then his face twisted viciously and he went for his gun. Brian got his out first and whipped it down. Asa was still bent forward and the gun barrel caught him across the back of the neck. He sprawled on his face.

Cameron cursed thickly and started to swing off his horse.

"Don't be a fool," Brian said. "Pick Asa up and put him on his horse."

Cameron stood by his fiddling animal, staring at Brian's gun. Brian put it away. Cameron's broad chest rose and fell with his angry breathing.

"I oughtta break you up," he said. "I oughtta break you up in little pieces."

"Slack off," Peters told him. "You know Brian was right."

Cameron did not move for another space, glowering at Brian from beneath his thick hedge of sun-whitened brows. At last he walked over to his unconscious brother. He picked Asa up like a baby and slung him on his belly across his saddle. Brian turned and dragged himself aboard his horse. The expenditure of emotion seemed to have drained him as much as the physical clash.

They pushed the herd across the basin, and found a blind canyon that would hold a hundred head of steers. They drove the cut in and Wirt Peters settled down at the mouth in the cover of some scrub oak. They found another box canyon and left that bunch with Cameron. Asa was still out cold and Cameron heaved him off his horse and stretched him flat on the ground with his saddle roll for a pillow. Sandoval had been studying Brian with a quizzical smile.

"Is funny," Sandoval said. "When this start, I think the boss I am."

It made Brian realize how, little by little, he had been assuming leadership. It had been an unconscious thing on his part. He hadn't been aware of its entire pattern until now.

"I didn't mean to take over, Chino."

The Yaqui shrugged. "Who's complaining?"

Brian grinned wearily at him. "Maybe you'd better give a few orders."

"*Bueno*. You take the scout. Get up high. See much. Come back at noon and I take over."

Brian nodded and turned back across the basin. In the first flush of sun the glens and canyons seemed pooled to the brim with a purple haze and the horizon was so mist-shrouded it was hard to tell where earth and sky met. He was across the basin and on the first shoulders of the Sierra Anchas when he saw the riders skylighted on a ridge above him. He pulled quickly into the cover of timber. He moved to the edge of a park where his view was not obscured. He could see the riders again, coming down off the ridge into timberline. There were three of them, too far away to recognize.

He realized his hand was on the butt of his gun and pulled it away with a soft curse. That wouldn't do him any good. What if they *were* Tarrant men? How could he stop them? He couldn't just murder them from ambush. And if he showed himself in any way it would tip his hand. He could think of no possible way to handle all of them. One at least would escape and bring the whole pack. It was what he had dreaded from the beginning of the drive.

They were passing him in timber now. He could hear their voices and the snorting of their horses at a distance. He moved cautiously to a new position and saw them across a last park below him, still headed for the basin. But they were close enough to recognize now. They were Kaibab and Stubs and a third horse runner named Bill who had worked off and on for the Double Bit.

He felt sick with relief. Then he realized how false that was. Latigo had been seen among the men who stampeded their cattle at Rabbit Sink. That meant the Double Bit was committed to Tarrant's wishes.

Brian saw the three men leave timber and drop into the basin. In a matter of minutes the lid would be off. They'd see the fresh cattle sign; they'd know Tarrant wasn't running any beef drive this far north and it would make them suspicious enough to investigate.

Driven by a sense of desperation, Brian put his horse down through the timber to intecept them. He came into the open when they were well into the basin but the sight of him checked them. He came up with them in a few minutes and saw that they had not reached the tracks of the herd yet. He halted his horse and greeted them. Kaibab touched his hatbrim silently. Stubs met his eyes, then looked aside, clearing his throat. The relationship of boss to hand was gone. They didn't know exactly how to treat him.

"Thought you was with Sandoval," Kaibab said.

Brian made a disgusted sound. "Who'd stay with him?"

"Where you bound?"

"Flagstaff maybe."

There was a silence. A wind boomed out of higher timber and rattled Kaibab's hatbrim. His narrow face was dark and sharp with suspicion.

"Hunting some green stuff?" Brian asked.

"Calf roundup was hard on the saddle strings," Kaibab said.

"Flushed some broomtails about dawn," Brian lied. "They headed west toward the Rim."

An eager light came to Stubs' eyes. "Big roan leader?"

"Yeah," Brian lied. "You after him?"

"We saw him through the glasses yesterday. Looked like a prime bunch of mares. Maybe we could run 'em down —"

Kaibab's sharp glance stopped Stubs. Kaibab's scarred hands fluttered on his reins and he looked across the basin toward the spur canyons in which the cattle were hidden.

"Glasses picked up something over there while we was up on the ridge. Get a bunch in one of those blind canyons, be like havin' 'em in a bottle."

"What bronc would be dumb enough to run in there?"

Something sly came into Kaibab's eyes. "Maybe Snakebite."

"Snakebite?"

"Yeah." The bronc-stomper squinted quizzically at Brian. "He's been seen around Red Bench this year. Couple of Seven Eleven hands told me he'd torn his saddle and bridle off somewhere. Meaner'n ever."

"And smarter'n ever," Brian said. "He wouldn't put himself in any blind canyon."

Kaibab was sardonic. "You seem so sure."

"That was some pronghorns your glasses picked up," Brian said. "I flushed 'em when I camped over there last night."

Stubs seemed convinced. He looked westward. "How far ahead of us would you say that roan is?"

"Half an hour. Moving easy."

"We're wastin' time," Stubs said.

Kaibab glanced obliquely at Brian. Then he held out his hand. Frowning, Stubs fumbled a pair of army binoculars from their case strapped to his saddle. He handed them to Kaibab. The bronc-stomper held them to his eyes and looked across the basin. Brian felt breathless and sick. Kaibab was studying a spur canyon farther north than the ones holding the cattle. But if he moved the glasses to the —

"See anything?" Stubs asked.

"Hell." Kaibab handed the glasses back.

"Let's go after the roan."

He looked at Brian, then reined his pied horse around and started west with Bill. Stubs seemed about to speak. An embarrassed look came to his face, he smiled sheepishly, touched his hatbrim, and followed the other two. Brian watched them for a few moments. Then he moved back the way he had come. He climbed to a ridge and watched the three riders till they were out of sight. He waited another hour but saw no sign of them circling back. Finally he crossed the basin again. At the head of one of the blind canyons he found Sandoval and Wirt Peters. He knew they must have seen his meeting with the Double Bit men.

"Well," Peters said. "If Asa was camped out there he would of given us away for good."

"You think Kaibab he know we're here?" Sandoval asked.

Brian shook his head. "I can't say."

"If he knew," Peters said, "would he tell?"

Brian frowned. "He was always a good hand."

"Take him a day to get in touch with anybody," Peters said. "Another day to get up here. Could we be in the Superstitions by then?"

"Drive like hell," Sandoval said. "Day and night."

"Can the cattle take it?"

"The cattle they can," Sandoval said. "If the men they can."

14

They pushed through the Sierra Anchas and down into Tonto. They knew what they were sacrificing, driving the cattle so hard. Every added mile meant that much more beef melted off the animals. But they couldn't help it. This was the last leg of the race against time.

The cattle were jumpy and frantic with exhaustion, ripe for a stampede. The men were half delirious with strain and weariness and lack of sleep. To Brian it was an insane nightmare of battling the wild and broken country, the intractable animals, his own deep need to lie down and sleep. But finally, like a ghostly wall rising out of the pale dawn mists, they saw the Superstitions ahead of them.

It was where Iguala left them. He was riding point and he stopped with that first early morning glimpse of the mountains. He pulled aside and let the herd stream past him. None of the men spoke as they passed him. This was a thing they had known from the beginning and they were too exhausted even to offer good-bys. As Wirt Peters passed, glancing at his man with

189

empty eyes, Iguala crossed himself.

They reached the Superstitions that day. They found a pass that rose into the gnarled peaks, winding and twisting until Brian could look back and see nothing but black-timbered slopes hemming him in on all sides. It filled him with the eerie sense of having cut himself off from all contact with the world he had known.

They pushed all that night to get as deep into the mountains as possible and stopped at dawn for their first real rest in days. Cameron took first watch on the herd while Pancho fixed their grub. Like sleepwalkers the men went through the motions of stripping their horses and setting out their bedrolls. Sandoval had dropped behind to cover their back tail and he rode in while they were eating.

"No sign of Tarrant," he said.

"Why should there be?" Asa said. "He's probably happy to see us get in here."

They all glanced at him sharply. Brian saw a haunted look come to Pancho's face. None of them spoke. Sandoval wheezed wearily, climbing off his horse, and stood leaning against it, his head bowed and his eyes closed. Asa looked around the circle of them, a wolfish defiance in his gaunt face, eyes fever-bright.

"We better get a man up on the ridge," Brian said.

Asa's head swung sharply to him. Then a completely wild look flamed into his eyes and he spat in the dirt at Brian's feet, flung his half-filled coffee cup from him, and rose and staggered to his bedroll, throwing himself face down on the blankets.

They all stared emptily at him. Sandoval was still leaning against his horse. He spoke in a feeble, wheezing voice.

"I can't do it, Brian. I just can't do it."

Brian couldn't eat any more. He sat there a long time, trying to gather enough will to rise. Finally he gained his feet and stumbled toward his horse. He got the saddle on somehow and laced it up. He tried three times before he got aboard. Peters had fallen asleep sitting cross-legged by the fire. His thin plate was still in his lap and his head was bent forward so far his hat had fallen off. Sandoval and Pancho watched Brian with glazed eyes as he turned his horse up the shoulder of the mountain and into timber.

He didn't know how long it took him to reach the ridge, pushing up through dense yellow pine and towering firs, his horse laboring in the thin air. But when he came out of the timber he could look down on a vast tumbled chain of mountains, their bases in the distance cloaked with a mauve vapor that made their timber-shrouded peaks seem completely severed from the earth, floating against the sky like disembodied spirits.

It brought back fragments of a hundred superstitions connected with these mountains. It nudged the primitive fears in him and apprehension eerie as a dog's seemed to lift the hackles of his neck. A weird hush lay over the scene. The motes swam like glittering gold through the channels of yellow sunlight in the timber-aisles and the heat rendered pitch from a thousand pines till its smell lay sweet as blackstrap on the air. It lent a cloying falseness to the lazy peace of the scene.

He hitched his horse in the trees and climbed to the ridgetop. He settled down to watch. But the need of sleep was like a sickness in him and he knew it would overpower him if he remained still long. He began to move around, keeping to cover, searching the tumbled and shadowy slopes beyond. All through the forenoon he fought off sleep until Peters came up to spell him. The man had lost twenty pounds in the drive and his once beefy jowls had sunk into the hollows under his cheekbones till his face had a gaunt, driven look.

"Funny," he said. "I heard about these mountains all my life. They're just like any other mountains."

"Yeah," Brian said. "They are."

Neither of them sounded convinced. Peters shifted in the saddle and the rigging groaned. It was the only sound in the world. "I wish it wasn't so quiet," he said. "I like to hear the birds singin'." Brian didn't answer. Peters squinted at him. "You want to watch that Asa," Peters said. "He's had a snake in him ever since you hit him."

Brian nodded. "I'll watch him."

When he reached camp Asa was still lying face

down in his blankets, sleeping heavily. Brian rolled in fully dressed and was asleep instantly. Sandoval woke him near dusk and they ate again and drove again. They drove through the night without incident but the pressure of waiting and watching was building up against all of them. They halted again and Pancho fixed breakfast and they fought sleep to eat it. When Sandoval was through he dumped his dishes in the wreck-pan and looked at Asa.

"Brian he's carried more than his load on watch," the Yaqui said. "This morning watch it's yours."

Asa's eyes swung to Brian, hot and smoldering. But they were all looking at Asa and the weight of their attention kept him quiet. With a bitter shape to his mouth, he rose and cinched up the saddle on his horse.

Brian turned in till midafternoon when Pancho waked him. He saddled a horse and rode up to the westward ridge where Sandoval was watching. The Yaqui said he had seen nothing.

"But the herd they are nervous. That I don't like." He put a sinewy hand on Brian's shoulder. "Apache I know. You got the bad watch. If they come, out of the sun it will be. Remember that. Out of the sun."

Brian nodded and watched Sandoval's blue roan switch its narrow rump back and forth down the steep pitch into timber. He thought of Sandoval's warning and looked at the sun. It lay westward just above the ridge and its fiery ball blinded him. The valley's shape disappeared and the tops of the countless trees became the silvery shimmer of a sea and his eyes began to water and he had to look away.

He hitched his horse in the timber below and climbed to the ridge. It was a hard climb in the thin air and he was breathing heavily and sweating when he reached the top. It started him itching all over again and he couldn't do anything but settle down in the rocks and scratch and rub himself like some mangy animal. He couldn't remember when he'd washed or had his clothes off; he had developed running sores from the friction of sweat-stiff clothes and when they had camped in the bottoms the mosquitoes had done their work. Remaining still like this only made the misery more acute.

He had a poor measure of the time he sat there, fighting sleep, trying to watch the endless miles of jagged country about him. The sun seemed to touch the top of the ridge now, a blazing core of fire that spilled its molten reflection down the ridge and into the timber. It was then, in his search of the shadowed valley below, that he saw the motion. He crawled deeper into the rocks and lay on his belly to watch.

It came again, a tawny flutter of motion in the lower timber. A clammy sweat moved down his back and the wind wouldn't dry it. He watched till he saw the motion again, higher now. It could be some animal.

He heard his horse snort below him and

turned to look on impulse. It swung his eyes into the sun that lay in a shattering explosion of light right on the top of the ridge. For a moment he was completely blinded. He closed his eyes, blinking them, and looked away from the sun down to where his horse was hitched. The animal was barely visible to him, deep in the timber, but he could hear it snorting and pulling at its hitch.

It increased the tension in him and he gripped his gun tighter as he looked back down the opposite slope. He saw the movement again. Closer. Much closer. It was no animal.

He inched his saddle gun forward, butt against his cheek, drawing a bead on them. The sun flashed against a bronze body. Another. Half a dozen of them, riding upward through the timber.

The horse snorted and fretted again below him. Could it smell them that far away? The Indians below had disappeared in shadow again. His finger was against the trigger. He knew his first shot would warn Sandoval and the others. Then what? Draw in to protect the herd. It was about all they could do. But at least they hadn't gone into it without warning.

The horse began to whinny and squeal and thrash around. It sounded frantic. He could ignore it no longer and turned for another look, squinting his eyes almost shut this time to blunt the sun's effect.

And knew what a fool he had been.

Watching the decoys on the slope below while the others came in from behind, came out of the sun as Sandoval had said, right out of the sun.

In that single instant before he went blind he had a dim impression of their movement coming down the top of the ridge with the blazing sun at their backs. He started to switch around in the rocks and work the lever on his gun but it was useless because he couldn't see anything.

He waited for them to fire but no shots came. And suddenly he understood. Their whole goal was to get him without noise so that the men in the valley would not be warned. And with that understanding he had his choice. If he stayed where he was he would have the protection and temporary safety of the rocks. But he would lose his chance to join Peters and the others with the herd.

With a soft curse he rose and lunged down the slope toward his horse. Still they did not fire. But a pair of bucks veered off the ridge. The sun was no longer at their back and he could see them. They were afoot. They were taking a chance too. They wanted that horse.

He knew what he would bring on him by shooting. But he had to get to the horse first. He threw his Winchester across his hip and fired. His second shot took the first running buck in the leg and the man pitched on his face and slid ten feet down the slope.

The others lost their need for silence then. The second running Indian began firing his long

Remington and those on the ridge started shooting.

A bullet kicked dirt high into the air behind Brian. He saw another bite bark out of a tree ten feet to the right. Then he was in the timber, a treacherous running target dodging through the densely massed trees. They protected him the same way they had his horse. He reached it and got the reins loose, throwing all his weight against them to hold the frantic animal. The second buck appeared, breech-clouted, moccasined. He had dropped his empty rifle and there was a knife in his hand.

Brian couldn't fire and mount at the same time. He swung aboard the horse. The Indian jumped at him. Brian swung his rifle at the man, caught him across the head. The Indian fell back but the jar took the rifle from Brian's hand. He heard the others coming into the trees and turned his horse and put the spurs to it.

His horse was wild and he couldn't hold it down. A dozen times he was almost swept off by the low branches. He came out into a park and had a glimpse of the valley below. Something was happening down there. A haze of dust hung thickly over the herd, hiding most of it from him. He had a vague glimpse of riders veering through the haze, the flash of gunfire.

Then he lost it as he plunged into timber again. It took him another ten minutes to reach bottom and when he came out of the trees the bulk of the herd was gone. He saw a few of them scattering into trees on the farther slopes and a small bunch running hell-for-leather back down the pass, but the rest of the herd was not even in sight.

There was a mass of twisted rocks farther up the pass. He could hear firing from there and saw movement in timber flanking the rocks. He plunged into the trees again, working his way cautiously toward the sound. His horse was lathered and blowing heavily, but as he neared the rocks the firing covered his sound.

Almost at the rocks, he caught sight of some Indians in timber on his flank. There were a dozen of them milling around on their ponies jabbering in guttural voices. Brian tried to dodge away but they caught sight of him and gave chase. All he could do now was put the spurs to his horse and run it headlong at the rocks. A wild volley of shots followed him, smashing through the pines overhead and spewing up handfuls of fallen needles from the carpet littering the ground.

Then he was in the open and the cattlemen began to fire from the rocks. It drove the Apaches back and kept them off his neck long enough for him to gain cover. The rocks broke from the slope in a natural fort, a strange twisted network of sandstone spires and towers and heaped boulders. He drove the laboring animal right into their midst and halted it among the men. They had their horses hitched in the hollow and were scattered out among the boulders, still firing. Sandoval ran from his nook to grab Brian's horse while he swung off. The Yaqui showed more emotion than Brian had ever seen before.

"Damn you," he said. He was grinning and he pounded Brian on the back. "I thought they got you, damn you —"

Though Sandoval had displayed a sort of casual comradeship during the cattle work this was the first indication of any true feeling he had shown Brian. It filled Brian with a warm affection for the dehydrated little Indian. Then both of them immediately sobered, as Peters came in from the rocks. He was bleeding from a cut on the face and limping heavily.

"They come in from behind us," Peters said. "Stampeded the herd. Too many to fight in the open."

The firing had stopped now. Brian looked at Asa and Cameron, sprawled down in the boulders heaped around the outer rims of the natural fort. Pancho was not in sight.

"He was keeping watch on the opposite ridge," Peters said. "That's where they hit us from. They must have got Pancho before he knew anything. He didn't give us no kind of warning."

Brian looked helplessly at the other wall of the valley, knowing how it must have happened with Pancho, giving him a decoy to watch while the others came out of the sun behind. Somehow Brian felt a deep guilt for the whole thing. If he had only heeded Sandoval's warning, if he hadn't been such a fool, watching these decoys below —

He saw that Asa was watching him. "Well, now what?" Asa asked sarcastically.

It was directed at Brian but Sandoval answered. "Maybe come night we get out."

"What about the cattle?" Asa asked.

The insolence of his tone angered Brian. "Maybe we can get 'em back yet," he said.

"I'd like to see that," Asa said.

"Don't make it tougher than it is," Peters said. He went back to the boulders and squirmed into them till he reached a position from which he could see the Indians. "There's a jag of 'em. I doubt if we can get out with our own hides."

Brian and Sandoval joined him. Sprawled among the boulders, sweating in the heat of a dying sun, Brian looked out at the timber and the parks and the open ground of the lower pass. There was still movement in the trees, the brazen flash of naked flesh, the shadowy passage of a horse. The Apaches had them completely surrounded and were keeping all the holes plugged. But the main group seemed to be gathering in the pass. There were perhaps twenty of them. Some of them sat tattered McLellan saddles and wore a motley collection of castoff army shirts and rawhide leggings and half-boots. But most of them were mounted on bareback ponies and were dressed in little more than G-strings and Apache war moccasins, worn up to the hip or folded over to knee height. They were a wild, mangy-looking lot but Brian could not see any war paint on their bodies. The bulk of them sat their fiddling ponies around a white-headed man, gesturing and talking excitedly.

Asa slid his rifle out. It was an old Ward-Burton bolt action. The Winchesters might not carry that far but the Indians were within range of the Ward-Burton.

"Don't be crazy," Peters said. "Kill a head man and they'll make sure we're all dead."

"On the other hand it might bust 'em up," Asa said. "You know how it is when their chief gets it."

He put his cheek against the butt. And an eddy of the crowd moved away from the white-headed Apache, revealing him fully to Brian for the first time.

Robles.

Brian pushed the gun aside so hard it hit Asa in the chin. The young man turned to him with a vicious curse.

"Damn you —"

"Slack off," Brian said. "Can't you see who it is?"

Still seething, Asa looked back at the Indians. Brian was staring at Robles. It had been a shock, recognizing the old man. Yet the logic of it took the shock away now. It was natural that Robles should come here. He was no reservation Indian. Brian remembered how often he had seen the old man staring off at these mountains, like a hound sensing something beyond human sight.

"What's the difference?" Asa asked.

"I can talk with him," Brian answered.

"They kill you," Sandoval said.

"They will anyway. Who's got something white?"

Peters had a white shirt on. They all looked at him. Finally he began to peel it off. He was sweating heavily and the heat had made his torso pink as rare steak. Brian took Peters' rifle from him and tied the shirt to its tip. Then he stood up and walked from the rocks. He saw the whole group of mounted Indians turn toward him and for just that moment he went sick with the anticipation of a gunshot.

But it did not come. He walked toward them. There was cotton in his mouth and tension made his hands ache on the rifle. He saw Robles staring at him and he took off his hat so the old man would see his red hair and know who it was. Robles seemed to lift in the saddle with the sight of that flaming mane. When Brian was halfway to them one of the Indians started to lift his gun. Robles caught his arm and stopped him.

The wind was against Brian and when he was close enough to smell the nitrogen reek of their hard-ridden ponies he stopped. A flurry of motion ran through the group — horses fiddling and fretting and men shifting in their saddles. There was a starved and bitter look to their hollow-cheeked faces. Their eyes had a mean agate-glitter.

"Can we talk?" Brian asked Robles.

The old man pressed his pinto with a knee and the horse walked to Brian. Robles still wore the faded purple shirt, the age-yellow buckskin leggings pouched at the knees. His face had aged; the countless pleats grooving his cheeks were edged with the silvery fur of senility. Yet his eyes were clear and bright.

"Why did you do this?" Brian asked. "We aren't here to harm you."

"You go through?"

It was strange to hear the old man's whispery voice after so long. It brought a flood of memory, a million fragments of Tiger, and softened Brian's voice as he spoke.

"We're driving to Alta."

"Others come."

"No. Just us."

"Others come."

Brian understood then what he meant. If the Apaches let this herd through it might open a route for further herds, then people wanting to settle. It would explode the mythical fear of the Superstitious and would rob this mangy, starved little band of their last refuge.

"Then the stories are true," Brian said.

Robles knew what he meant. The Indian glanced around at the other Apaches. "No," he said.

"But the men who disappeared in here?"

"Men die in Sierra Anchas. No Apaches there."

Brian looked at the Indians, sullen, hostile, like a pack of curs waiting to jump. Robles saw the disbelief in Brian's face. The ancient Apache looked at the tumbled, haze-ridden peaks east of them.

"Man get lost back there easy. No food. No water." Something close to a smile touched his face, holding a wise and aged bitterness. "Other ways to die. Two gold hunters, last year. They find the gold. Each want too much. Kill each other."

"But that can't account for all of it."

"You ever see?"

Brian frowned dubiously, realizing how intangible the evidence had always been. The Superstitions had been such a place of mystery for so long that it had become traditional to assign any unexplained violence to them. A man was burned out of his homestead and it was supposed to be a raiding band of Apaches. A man was found dead in the desert and it came from the Superstitions.

But now Brian was shaken. He had never known Robles to lie. "The rustling," he said. "So much of it was supposed to come from here."

"Why we go outside? We have all we can eat. Water. Earth. Sky. Enough for us."

"Then the bad sign you were always talking about."

"Not from here."

"Did you know that at the time?"

Robles shook his head. "I know nothing then. I just feel. Bad sign. Some kind of bad sign."

Brian remembered how he had scoffed at Robles' talk. Now he was more willing to believe. "If it didn't come from here —"

"Tarrant," Robles said.

It checked Brian for a moment. Yet it was no surprise. He knew now that the Tarrant faction had probably been working for a long time to undermine the Double Bit and get Tiger into a position where he would have to do their bidding. Tiger's death had merely shifted their attention to Brian, and Brian's weaknesses had played right into their hands. But all of Tarrant's activity had been gradual, undercover, shadowy. It was logical that Robles, with his primitive sensitivity to the slightest change in the country, should have sensed something wrong without being able to pin it down.

"That time we found Nacho with the Double Bit cattle," Brian said.

Robles nodded. "Part of it. Nacho say he work for Latigo. He say truth."

Brian leaned forward. "You mean Latigo was in it even then?"

"All the time. Latigo work for Tarrant."

It brought another piece to the picture. It made Brian realize how the Double Bit had actually been bled dry of beef. Apparently his profligacy had little to do with it. Robles told him that Latigo and Nacho had been working at it through the years. The cattle run off by Nacho had been attributed to the Apaches in the Super-stitions or the small-time border-hoppers. Latigo had stood ready to cover Nacho should he be discovered, as he was when Tiger and Brian had come up with him. At the same time, by falsifying the tally books, Latigo had covered the depletion of the herds.

At the same time, Robles said, Latigo was responsible for the loss of cattle by the Salt Rivers. One of their greatest strengths had lain in the mutual trust between the Salt Rivers and Tiger Sheridan. But if the Salt Rivers thought the Double Bit was mixed up in the unusual drift of their cattle onto the Rim, that trust would be undermined and finally ruined by a corroding suspicion. It was only one of the many ways Tarrant had worked to ruin the Salt Rivers, weaken the Double Bit, and gain the upper hand. Brian wanted to spit.

"You found this out, here?" he asked.

Robles nodded. "These people know what happen. Better than anybody. Like in the old days. A snake crawl a hundred miles away. Apache know."

But it had been too late to help. Brian knew that. By the time Robles had discovered the truth, they had already smashed Brian. He looked at the line of dark faces. They were growing restless, muttering among themselves, jerking at their fretting ponies.

"And you're saying they've stayed back in here

all these years?" Brian said. "They haven't raided, they haven't rustled, they haven't been responsible for the men who disappeared in here?"

"Sometimes they kill. Only to save themself."

"I could almost believe you, except for today."

"You shoot first."

Brian had to admit that. His face grew grim. "What about Pancho?"

Robles lifted a veined hand in a signal. The ranks parted and the Mexican was led forward by a pair of riders. He walked between them, hands tied behind him. He was sweating and his eyes rolled in his head.

"Dios de mi vida," he said. *"Ruegue por mi alma, Señor Brian, lastima de Dios —"*

"Settle down, Pancho," Brian said. "I think it's all right." The man subsided and Brian spoke to Robles. "What do you want, then?"

"Take your cattle. Go back."

"You know we can't. This is our last chance."

"If you get through, others come."

"If we get through we'll stand a chance against Tarrant. And if we beat him nobody else will drive cattle through here. I give you my word."

Robles was silent a long time, studying Brian. Finally he asked, "Coming through here. Your idea?"

Brian knew the whole thing hung in precarious balance now. He couldn't sense what Robles was diriving at, and hesitated with his answer. It made Robles look at Pancho. The Mexican nodded vehemently.

"*Si, si, Señor* Brian's idea —"

Robles looked at Brian. "You think we kill you?"

Brian grinned ruefully. "I guess I believed the stories."

"And still you come."

Brian nodded. Robles looked at Brian's hands, callused and scarred and crisscrossed with rope burns. He looked at Brian's clothes, tattered and filthy. Finally he looked at Brian's face. Weather and work had taken all the youth from it. There was no softness of flesh to hide the raw and shining ridges of cheekbone and jaw. The eyes were narrowed habitually against the sun now and a fine netting of wrinkles was forming at their tips. Where dust didn't cover the skin it showed a burn as dark as Robles' face and a hard fighting shape had come to the lips. Finally Robles wheeled his horse and walked back to the Apaches. He began talking in their guttural tongue. It started a big argument. A half-naked buck moved his horse till he was knee-to-knee with Robles, talking viciously, making wicked slicing gestures with one hand at Brian. The others set up a monkey-like jabbering.

Robles held up his hand and finally silenced them. He began an oration. By the way they listened Brian could see the power the old man had gained over them. Pancho stood between the two riders who had led him to the front, breathing heavily, working his mouth. Finally

Robles stopped. There was silence for a while. Then one man answered from the group. It was just a couple of words. The buck who had argued with Robles pulled away from the old man, and Brian couldn't tell whether it was triumph or defeat on his face. Robles turned his pony and came back. He came up to Brian and put a hand on his shoulder.

"We decide," he said. "We take your word. You go on through. We help you get cattle back in bunch."

15

It took them a week to reach Alta, driving by day now, going easier on the cattle and on themselves. They were conscious of being watched as long as they were in the mountains but saw no more of the Indians till the last day. It was sunset and they were trailing out of the last canyon onto the flats of the desert. Brian looked back and saw a figure sitting a horse on a westward bluff, white-headed, lonely, as much a part of the land and sky as the rocks or the wind. Brian raised his hand and Robles lifted his in answer.

Brian had the impulse to ride up and speak again with the old Indian. But in the next moment Robles was gone. Brian understood then. This had been his benediction, in a way, and it was as much as he would get from the old man. Their relationship had changed. Robles had seen something new in Brian — perhaps the manhood he had always looked for — and had acknowledged it by letting Brian take the herd through. But that was as far as it could go. Robles had come here to stay and to die. He had said good-by and further words would have added little. It was his stoic way and Brian had to accept it. But it was like brushing his fingers against something in the night — a sense of finding something and losing it all in an instant. Filled with intangible sadness, he turned his horse back to the herd.

It was the wrong time of year for a beef drive and they got a poor quotation on their cattle at Alta. But they had expected that and it did not dim their triumph. They got one hotel room and slept out a night and a day, four of them lying crosswise on the bed and the other two in their saddle rolls on the floor. Then they had themselves a big drunk. And then they started back to Mescal Springs.

It was a bad ride through the desert. They found none of the Tarrant men at the waterholes they would have used on this route. There was barbed wire around several of the sinks and signs of a camp near by. Rabbit Sink was deserted. The corral they had used still stood, occupied now by nothing but the rotting carcasses of the cattle that had died there. Five days out of Alta they reached Sandoval's place, exhausted and triumphant.

Morton Forge was the first one they saw. He was coming from one of the bear-grass huts as they crossed the trickle of brackish water seeping out of the springs. With a whoop he ran heavily toward them.

"Dammit," he shouted. "We thought you'd been lost in those Superstitions for good."

He ran among them, slapping at their saddles, pulling on their arms, shaking hands all around. When he heard they had gotten the cattle through he was even more excited.

"You get as much credit as us," Brian said. "Looks like you kept those Tarrant hands tied down a long time."

Forge chuckled. "I never saw such a bunch of sitting ducks. I kept trailing those cattle in and out every day. Finally they must of come in close enough to see what they was watching. I found their tracks real close the next morning and —"

He broke off, looking toward the house, and his humor fled. Brian saw that Estelle had stepped from the door. Her hair was a golden glow in the fading light. The expression on Forge's face made Brian ask:

"What's the matter?"

"I guess you better know," Forge said. "Pa's pretty bad. We had to call the doctor."

It was like a chill running through Brian. He turned his horse up to meet Estelle as she hurried from the house. The other riders followed, with Forge trailing on foot. Brian stopped his gaunted horse by the girl and she reached up to grasp his arm. For a moment her pleasure at his return filled her face.

"Brian," she said. Her voice was husky and seemed to tremble a little. "We didn't know . . . you have no idea . . . it's so good to have you back."

"We got the cattle through," he said. He knew

212

she'd want to hear that. He dismounted stiffly and stood with his back against the horse looking at her. "Forge told us about Pa."

It had become an effort to retain her smile and she didn't try any longer. She let him see the trouble like shadows in her eyes and then she looked down at her clasped hands.

"He's a little better since the doctor came." She took a quick little breath. "He'll want to see you."

They walked together to the house. He kept looking at her. He couldn't help it. There was something like a hunger in him, a hunger he hadn't really known was there till now. It was like seeing her for the first time. At the door she became aware of it and she stopped, raising her head in a quick response. Their eyes met. They were on the edge of something again. She moistened her lips.

"Do you want to go in?"

Her voice sounded thick. He hesitated a moment longer, then ducked into the house. Sandoval's wife was bent over the stew kettle. She wheeled at their entrance; when she saw Sandoval following Brian her fat moon face began to shine. Sandoval went to her and took her by the arm. Their eyes met and he grinned sheepishly and squeezed her arm.

"Old woman," he said gruffly.

Pa lay on the same pallet against the wall. The ravages of fever and pain had turned his head to a sunken skull. His roached hair had begun to grow out and it lay in a tangled gray mat against the pillow. Asa cursed softly and went to one knee by his father. The bitterness was gone from the youth's face; its edges were softened by troubled concern and unashamed affection. He put a hand on Pa's shoulder. The man's eyes opened, fever-filmed, wild-looking. When he saw Asa he tried to smile and his hand came from beneath the covers like a claw, seeking Asa's.

"We got 'em through," Asa said. "Tarrant hasn't licked us yet."

"Good boy." Pa moistened cracked lips, trying to smile, and his eyes moved around their faces. "Good boy."

He sighed, as if the small effort had exhausted him, and closed his eyes. Asa got to his feet. He looked at Brian, as if seeking help. For that moment all the antagonism was gone from between them and Brian found it hard to remember how he had clashed with this youth. Asa's eyes dropped and he ran a hand through his tousled hair.

"Well — what now?"

"You've got to eat and rest," Estelle said.

They did not respond. Sandoval was looking at Pa. "When was doctor here?"

"Yesterday."

"Then Tarrant knows," Cameron said. "Everybody knows."

"And the weak ones will be jumping over the line," Peters said. "There won't be any Salt River party left."

"We still have a chance," Brian said. "Getting these cattle through proves we can buck Tarrant. It might hold us together."

"Without a leader?"

"Choose a new leader. What's wrong with Sandoval? He's got enough guts to hang on a fence."

"Better face it," Sandoval said. "Not many of these men they will take orders from an Indian."

Peters looked at Asa. "The Gillette name still has a lot of pull."

Brian knew a deep reluctance to let either Asa, with his hot head and his thoughtless impulses, or Cameron take the reins. It must have shown in his face for some of the defiance returned to Asa.

"It was your idea," he said.

Brian said, "Why not make nominations and let them put it to a vote?"

Forge nodded. "We'd better call a meeting right away, if we want anybody left."

"If we ride right now we could get most of them here late tonight," Asa said.

"You can't," Estelle said. "You've been in the saddle all day."

"No time to waste," Sandoval said. "If we do it, we got to do it now."

They ate first. Then, exhausted as they were, they went to the corrals to rope out fresh horses. Estelle went along to help saddle up. Brian had to pick a roan that had some vinegar to spill; it fought him around the corral and he was the last to leave. With the others gone, Estelle held the excited horse while he put the tack on. With the girth cinched up, he took the reins from her hands. She was smiling at him.

"You're really an all-around hand now."

"I guess I've learned a lot," he said.

"And changed a lot."

He did not answer for a moment. It was something he had felt himself, something he had seen in Robles's reaction. The external change was obvious enough. The calluses on his hands, the burn on his face, the muscles in his belly. Yet there was more than that, something still occurring inside, shadowy, as yet hard to define. The old restlessness was gone, the sense of futility and frustration. Perhaps that was a part of it. He'd needed something to fight for.

More and more he felt a kinship with these people, a sense of belonging that he'd never known before. He was a part of something bigger than himself and it seemed to give him the roots and the core he had lacked before.

"Do you like the change?" he asked.

"I'd say so," she said.

They were close again, speaking in low voices, with that thing tingling between them. The dusk made shadowy curves of her body. The hunger was in him again and he could deny it no longer. He took her face in his hands and kissed her. She met it with her lips full and soft. She didn't pull away or move closer. Yet there was no withholding. Her giving was complete. Through his hands he could feel the faint trembling of her body as he pulled back to look at her face. Her eyes were half closed. She was breathing heavily and in her shining face was an awakening.

"It's strange," she whispered. "I wanted you to do that."

His own body was trembling and his face felt hot and there was a drumming pulse in his temples. They were the familiar signs, yet all of it was altered by some subtle alchemy into something far apart from the passion he had known for Arleen. He had the sense of holding something fragile in his hands and he felt that if he said the wrong thing or made the wrong move he would shatter it.

She must have taken his silence for something else. The shimmer left the surface of her eyes. "Arleen?" she asked.

It seemed to take the bottom out of everything. He hadn't been thinking of Arleen when he kissed Estelle, hadn't been conscious of anything but his own burning needs. He released her and stepped back. He smiled ruefully.

"I guess I have changed," he said. "A few months ago I could have laughed it off."

She did not answer. Then he turned and stepped into the saddle. He sat heavily there, brooding down at her. At last, seeing he had no answer for her, all the life went out of her face.

"I'm sorry, Estelle," he said. "I guess I had no right."

Without speaking, she turned and went

toward the house. Miserable with the confusion in him, he watched her till she was but a blur in the distance. Then he touched heels to the nervous horse and passed into the night.

They had each taken a different section of the country below the Rim. Brian picked up Ring Partridge and a man named Sam Fallon. They got back to Mescal Springs about ten o'clock to find most of the other Salt Rivers there, gathered around a blazing fire in front of the bear-grass huts. Brian and the other two dismounted on the fringe of the group and he saw that Asa stood before the fire, speaking hotly to the men.

"This drive proves we can buck Tarrant. If we can do it once we can do it again . . ."

As Asa went on, blond-bearded Wirt Peters saw Brian and moved over to speak in a low tone. "Most of 'em are here. It looks like the Gillette name still means something. They don't think Cameron's got enough drive, but they're willing to let Asa rod the show."

Sam Fallon pushed his way toward the center, a stooped little man with a nasal voice. "Tarrant's bought up a lot of those notes Sheridan used to hold. He's threatening to foreclose now unless I put my name on that recall petition."

The crowd turned toward him and Asa asked, "Can't you hold out a few weeks? This may be the turning point."

"A man's got to think of his family," Fallon

said. "My wife's due for another baby. We ain't got no place to go."

"And what about them as still has a herd to think of?" a man named Rados asked. "Tallow Creek's gone bone dry. The only way I can save my stock is to use Red Sinks. Tarrant's offered 'em to me if I go with him."

Brian began moving toward the center. He could see Asa's temper mounting and knew what was coming. Asa shouted back at them, "Then why don't you all just jump right in Tarrant's wagon?"

Sheriff Cline caught his arm. "That ain't no way to talk, son —"

Asa wheeled toward the paunchy lawman. "Why should I listen to you? Tarrant has you in the hollow of his hand."

Cline shook his massive gray head. "You know I didn't have anything to do with foreclosing on you. It was Nacho, while I was chasing those Apaches that jumped the reservation."

"Which puts Tarrant's brand on Nacho too."

Asa tried to wheel back and speak to the crowd but Cline kept the hold on his arm, saying angrily, "That's not true —"

With an angry curse, Asa tore his arm free. The motion flung it outward and across Cline's face. The sheriff staggered backward and then caught himself. His broad-jowled face went gray with rage and humiliation. Tears from the blow across his nose squeezed out from the tips of his squinted eyes and he spoke in a shaken voice.

"You young fool —"

Brian saw that Asa was ready to lunge at the man and he stepped between them, grabbing Asa's arm. The youth tried to tear free, a wild look to his face, but Brian hung on.

"Slack off, Asa. Do you want to tell Pa you tore the whole thing apart the first night?" It checked Asa for a moment. He stood rigidly, nostrils pinched and white. Brian went on: "You got the guts to lead us. I know that. But you've got to keep your head."

Mayor Prince moved in close to them, portly, white-headed, placating. "He's right, Asa. A leader's job is to hold things together. It's what made Pa so valuable to us."

Brian had seen the youth's deep affection for his father, in Sandoval's house, and knew it was the one thing that might touch Asa. "You can't let Pa down," he said.

Asa's face went slack and the tension left his body. His shoulders bowed and he ran his sinewy hand through matted black hair, shaking his head. "All right," he said. "I apologize, Cline."

The sheriff made a grumbling sound, rubbing his nose. Sandoval stepped close to Asa, speaking in a low voice.

"Is the weak ones we got to hold. If they go, it start the bust-up. Tell Fallon I cover his mortage with money from the drive. Rados can water his cattle at the springs here till fall roundup."

Asa nodded, turned, passed on Sandoval's

offer. Fallon shook his head dubiously.

"It's a generous offer, Chino. What do we gain by it?"

"Time. Time to fight the recall."

"Ain't that a losing battle? Councilman Lewis claims he overheard the division superintendent offer Prince a cut of the freight rates if Prince saw that the franchise came through." Fallon wouldn't look at Mayor Prince when he said it.

"What kind of trumped-up charge is that?" Brian answered. "Tarrant couldn't possibly make it stick unless the Salt Rivers were too whipped to fight it."

"We can lick him on this franchise," Asa said. "A railroad in Apache Wells would make you all a dozen times bigger than you are — big enough to stop Tarrant for good."

Morton Forge began to chuckle. "It sounds like it's worth fighting for."

"You'll do it?" Asa asked.

Forge looked around at the others, getting a nod from each man. "We'll do it," he said.

16

The meeting broke up after midnight and Brian went to bed with the feeling that they had patched things up for at least the present. He slept late and woke near noon to find himself alone in the beargrass hut. He dressed and went out to see Sandoval, Cameron, and Pancho eating breakfast in the shade of the *ramada* by the main house. Estelle must have seen him from inside for as he reached the house she appeared with a cup of coffee.

"Thanks," he said. "Where's Asa?"

A shadow was between them, since their meeting the night before. She seemed withdrawn before him and unusually sober. "Fallon came from Prince this morning," she said. "Mayor Prince wanted to see Asa."

She went back inside. Brian asked Sandoval, "What's it about?"

The Yaqui shook his head. "We was still asleep. I guess Prince didn't say."

Estelle brought Brian a plate of food in a few minutes. He sat on one of the split logs by the door to eat. After he finished, Sandoval rolled a pair of cigarettes and offered one to Brian. They sat side by side, smoking, silent. Brian was still stiff and sore and beaten from the grueling ride behind them. He didn't want to think. He didn't want to move. The somnolent sounds of chickens scratching and clucking in the door-yard made him sleepy and he dozed in the shade, dropping his cigarette half-smoked.

The trembling of the earth woke him. The sun stood in the middle of the sky, pouring a steel-bright heat on the land. Morton Forge was bringing a hard-ridden horse across the waters of the seep. The men under the *ramada* jumped to their feet and ran toward him. He hauled the lathered animal up, shouting to be heard over the roar of its breathing.

"Things have blowed up in our faces. Asa's gone and killed Sheriff Cline!"

The blood drained from Brian's cheeks. His weight settled against the earth like a man recovering from one blow and setting himself against the next.

"Nacho and Harv Rich brought Cline's body to town about ten o'clock," Forge said. "They had Asa with 'em. Claimed they saw him shoot Cline."

"Saw him?"

"That's the story. A couple more bronc Apaches jumped reservation yesterday. Cline got a tip they'd been seen in Silver Sinks. Neither of his deputies had checked in. He left word for them to follow him. They claim they was up

223

on the rim when they saw Cline get it."

Silently, helplessly they stared at each other. They all knew what it meant. Cline had been loved and respected throughout the county. With Asa as their newly chosen leader, the Salt Rivers couldn't help but share the blame for Cline's murder. It would wipe out what support Prince had left both in and out of the council, and ruin his last chance for pushing the franchise through."

"*Dios,*" Sandoval said. "I feel like somebody he kick me in the stomach."

"Cline and Harv Rich and Nacho and Asa all in Silver Sinks at the same time," Brian said musingly.

"Natural Asa'd be there," Cameron said. "He'd have to go through the sinks on his way to Prince's."

Sandoval was frowning at Brian. "What you think?"

"I think it's a helluva coincidence," he said. None of them answered. The horse snorted and wheezed. Finally Brian said, "Well, whatever happened, Asa's going to need the best lawyer we can get." They were all frowning at him and he knew they were thinking of the same man he was. His chin lifted defiantly. "Damn it," he said. "It's worth a try, isn't it?"

None of them responded. He went into the corral and started roping out the line-back. Cameron walked heavily up to the house and Brian knew he was going to tell Estelle. While

Brian was saddling up, she came down to the corral. Her face was white and strained. She stopped by the horse, made a couple of false starts, then said:

"Brian . . . do you think Asa really did it?"

He shook his head. "I don't know."

"You hate him, don't you?"

He shook his head. "No, Estelle. We've fought a lot. But he's just a kid with a bad temper. Give him a chance, he'll find himself. He'll be all right."

"I want to go."

He nodded grimly. "All right. Cameron and I'll hitch our horses behind the buckboard."

It was a long ride into town. None of them spoke much. They were all bitterly shocked and discouraged by this new blow and Brian was intensely conscious of the strain between him and Estelle, shadowing every glance, every word. They reached Apache Wells in the afternoon.

The jail stood on West Cochise, across the creek from the more respectable part of town, a long crumbling adobe building shaded by a ragged line of willows that set up a melancholy whisper against its roof whenever the wind moved their thin foliage. At the door a group of idlers surrounded Nacho, who sat in a chair tilted back against the wall, rolling a cigarette and talking expansively. They all turned as the wagon rattled up out of the creek, and Nacho came to his feet. Brian and Cameron got down, helping Estelle to the ground.

"Nobody goes in here," Nacho said. "Court order."

Brian faced him. "Show me the order."

Nacho began to leer. "Old Double Bit, he's getting tough."

"Show me the order, Nacho, or get out of the way."

Nacho dropped his cigarette and stepped on it. The idlers began to back off. "You want to be in there with Asa?" Nacho asked.

Brian's weight settled against his toes but Estelle grabbed his arm, stopping him. "There's been enough trouble," she said. She turned to Nacho. "Please — what harm can we do by seeing him?"

Nacho did no answer. He merely looked at her. It was the same look that every idler in front of every saloon gave every woman that passed on the street. Color rushed into Estelle's cheeks. An angry reaction ran through Brian but before he could move Estelle made an exasperated sound and darted around Nacho. He caught her, trying to spin her back. She bit his hand. With a howl of pain he released her. She wheeled and ran into the jail.

"You little bitch," Nacho shouted. Holding his hand, he lunged after her. Brian followed, catching him by the arm just inside the door and wheeling him back. Nacho tore free, his face vicious and white. His hand was on his gun when somebody called sharply from outside.

"Nacho!"

The breed checked his motion, staring past Brian. A tall white-headed man in a frock coat parted the knot of watchers with the tip of his gold-headed cane and stepped to the door.

"Mr. Sheridan has a perfect right to see the prisoner, Nacho," he said. "You're taking your duties a little too seriously, I believe."

It was Harold Parrish, the circuit judge from Alta. Nacho subsided, the color returning to his face and rendering it dark and sullen. Brian relaxed, grinning wryly at Parrish.

"Thanks, Judge."

Parrish nodded soberly and Brian turned, followed by Cameron, to walk into the dank cell-block. Brian saw Estelle talking with Asa in the last cell and he couldn't help grinning wryly to himself. He'd always known she had spunk but he'd never seen it so graphically displayed. She was still breathing heavily, excited color in her cheeks. She turned as they came up, speaking breathlessly.

"Asa says he didn't do it, Brian."

Asa stood at the door, lean hands clenched around the bars. In his gaunt face, already edged with a stubble beard, was nothing but defiance for Brian. Cameron saw the bitter expression and spoke with a heavy exasperation. "You got to quit fighting Brian, Asa. He's here to help you. He didn't have to come at all."

Asa's eyes tried to hold the defiance. But they shifted in confusion and he looked down at the floor. Some of the hostility drained from him.

He ran a hand nervously through his black hair.

"What happened?" Brian said.

"Sam Fallon came early this morning," Asa said. "Told me Prince wanted to see me. Something about the franchise. Urgent. Fallon dropped off at his place and I went on through Silver Sinks. It was the quickest route to the mayor's. In the sinks I heard this shot. I got off my horse and went through the rocks. I came on Cline's body. That's where Nacho and Harv Rich found me. Now Fallon's saying he didn't come this morning. None of you saw him. I can't prove anything."

Estelle shook her head helplessly. "The whole thing's so crazy."

"And so neat," Brian muttered.

Estelle looked at him, eyes pleading. "You believe Asa?"

Brian said, "Sam Fallon was the weakest one last night. Could be he went straight to Tarrant about our meeting."

"And they knew I'd take Silver Sinks to Prince's," Asa said.

They were silent. Finally Brian grinned at Asa, trying to be reassuring. "Take it easy. We'll break it. If it's humanly possible, we'll break it."

Asa answered the grin, a little sheepishly. "Damn my temper anyway, Brian. I've been wrong from the beginning. Is there any way we can wipe it off and start over?"

"Easiest thing in the world," Brian said.

He put out his hand. Asa stuck his through the

bars and they shook, grinning at each other for a moment. Then the humor left them. Brian looked at Estelle. She made a helpless sound. Brian looked once more at Asa, reached through to give him a reassuring punch on the shoulder, then went out. Parrish was in the office, going over the docket with Nacho and the bailiff.

"We've set the trial for this Saturday," he told them.

"Isn't that a little soon?" Brian said.

Parrish shook his head. "I've got a big circuit, Mr. Sheridan. If we don't get started on this as soon as possible I'll have to set it over till next year."

More discouraged than ever, they left the jail and rode back across the creek to the main part of town. Brian stopped at Wolffe's office, but the door was locked. When he came back downstairs the banker's kid was talking with Estelle. He told them Wolffe was at the Double Bit. Estelle was looking back toward the jail.

"I hate to leave Asa here alone. That Nacho —"

She trailed off. Cameron nodded. "I feel the same way. If Tarrant did this there's no telling how much farther he'll go."

"We could stay in town," Estelle said. "Take rooms at the hotel."

It would be more a gesture than anything else, but Brian sympathized with her need to watch over Asa. "I'll leave you here then," he said. "I want to see Wolffe."

It was a long, hot ride to the Double Bit and Brian had to push his horse to make it before evening. He thought the first sight of the ranch would hurt — the myriad windows flashing in the coppery glow of the sun, the barns and corrals backed up into the mist-purple foothills. But somehow he was filled with no hurt, no sense of loss. As he dismounted in front of the house he saw a man coming from the barns. It was Latigo, and the man reached the porch before Brian. He tucked his thumbs into the waistband of his Levis, eyes measuring Sheridan insolently.

"Is Wolffe here?" Sheridan asked.

"No."

"Jigger told me he was."

"He ain't!"

"Who is?"

"Me."

Brian started onto the porch. "I'll see for myself."

Latigo made a sharp shift to block his way. "No, you won't. If Wolffe was in, he wouldn't want to see you."

Brian stared at him, seeing the thinly veiled contemp in the man's eyes. "I'm going in, Latigo."

Latigo's lips peeled back in a wolfish smile. "Like you took the Steeldust away from me in Apache Wells?"

Brian hung a moment longer, meeting the man's stare. Then he lunged in at an angle, as if trying to get around one side of Latigo. The foreman shifted hard that way to block him.

Brian stopped at the last instant. It left Latigo plunging forward without anything to block. He tried to catch himself, but it was too late. His impetus had carried him by Brian at an angle.

Brian hit him across the side of the neck, jack-knifing him and knocking him off his feet. The man rolled over into the compound and came to his hands and knees. Brian moved at him. Latigo came up off his hands and knees, throwing himself at Brian's midsection.

Brian went into him, slamming an uppercut into his face. The blow and the smashing force of Brian's body pitched Latigo over backward. He flopped over in the dirt a second time, staring up at Brian with a mixture of pain and surprise in his face.

With a gutteral sound, Latigo switched around and scrambled to his feet. Brian rushed him. Latigo ducked his first blow, feinting at Brian's face. Brian threw up an arm to block it. The real blow hit Brian in the solar plexus.

He couldn't help doubling over in pain. He felt Latigo cup those hands behind his neck. Felt the man's weight shift to slam a knee into his face.

He jerked aside in the last instant and caught the knee and heaved.

It pitched Latigo over on his back again. The blow dazed him and he shook his head before he rose again. Brian lunged in as soon as Latigo gained his feet. Latigo blocked his first blow and counterpunched for his solar plexus again. This time it struck Brian in the ridged muscle of his belly. Six weeks ago it would have doubled him over anyway. Now he only grunted and struck back. The blow rocked Latigo's hand. He feinted at Latigo's belly. The man hugged his arms in and left his face open. Brian hit him in the face. Latigo went down so hard it knocked the air from him with a sick grunt.

He lay on his belly a long time before rolling over. He finally raised his head, trying to see Brian through the blood streaming into his eyes. His breathing had a broken sound.

"You'd better not get up again," Brian said. "You're whipped and you know it."

Latigo hung his head, spitting blood into the dirt. "Damn you," he said. "Damn you."

Brian waited till he was sure the man would not get up. Then he turned to go inside. As he did so the front door was opened and Wolffe stepped out, followed by Ford Tarrant. Anger settled its pale grooves about Wolffe's thin-lipped mouth with the sight of Latigo on the ground, and his boots beat a swift tattoo as he crossed the porch.

"We thought somebody was busting a bronc," he said. His intense black eyes fixed accusingly on Brian. "What's going on?"

"Latigo thought you didn't want to see me," Brian said. "I changed his mind."

"See me about what?"

Brian glanced at Tarrant before answering.

There was something vaguely subservient in the way Tarrant stood at Wolffe's elbow, partially behind the man. His face was unusually florid and Brian knew he had been drinking. Brian thought he would meet a strong hostility from the man, now that they had clashed in open warfare. But there was a cloudy indecision in Tarrant's eyes, as though he still didn't know quite what role to assume with Brian.

"What are you doing here?" Brian asked.

Tarrant tried to bluster. "I don't see that it's any of your —"

"He came to tell me about Cline," Wolffe said, breaking in impatiently.

"That's why I came too," Brian said. "I'm asking you to defend Asa."

Tarrant could not hide his surprise, and Wolffe scowled deeply at Brian. "With all the evidence against him?"

Brian looked directly at Tarrant. "What if we could prove he didn't do it?"

Tarrant's face went wooden. He couldn't avoid the brittle tone of his voice. "You have evidence?"

"Maybe."

"If you've got it, come out and say so," Wolffe said irritably. "Otherwise you're talking supposition —"

"I'm talking friendship, George."

"Asa was never my friend."

"I was." Brian moved closer to Wolffe, standing a foot from him. "You can't sit on the fence forever, George. You know what Ford tried to do with Sandoval's cattle —"

"Self-protection," Tarrant said thickly.

"The hell with that," Brian said. His anger was rising. "A man's got a right to live. You can't have it all, Ford." He turned to Wolffe. "A man's life is at stake. An innocent man. You've got to come down off the fence, George."

"Brian, I can't —"

"Then you're with Tarrant. That's what you're saying, isn't it?"

"Brian, how can you — ?"

"It's one way or the other!" In his anger at the man, in his furious need to sway him and convince him, Brian caught him by the lapels. "Can't you see that? Either you're with us or you're against us, George. It can't be any other way."

Wolffe caught Brian's arm, struggling to twist free. "Let go, you young fool —"

"Are you saying you won't do it?"

"I already told you —"

Brian gave vent to his boiling anger with a curse, shoving Wolffe violently backward. The man tripped on the edge of the porch and fell heavily. Latigo was on his feet, and he made an involuntary move behind Brian.

Brian pivoted toward him. The man stopped his motion, face still bloody and mottled with dirt. He was unarmed and he glanced at the gun holstered against Brian's hip. Brian half turned again toward Wolffe. The man was getting to his feet, his face a white mask of fury and humiliation.

"You shouldn't have done that." His voice trembling and a smoldering, vindictive rage glowed in his black eyes. "I'll smash you for good this time."

Brian stared blankly at him. "*This* time?"

Wolffe sent a contemptuous glance at Tarrant. "You don't think it was that weasel, do you?"

"George!" Tarrant's protest was panicky.

"I *want* him to know," Wolffe said hotly. "He's kicked his dog for the last time."

"So you drag the rest of us down with you," Tarrant said.

"Nobody's dragging you down!" Wolffe said disgustedly. Brian stared at them blankly, his mind turned momentarily blank by the shock of what he'd heard, trying helplessly to piece together the implications. Like a detached observer, he watched the quarrel reach a crest between the two men, sensing that it was a culmination of earlier clashes.

"Then why not go on?" Tarrant swayed faintly and his slack lips were twisted in a drunken sneer. "Why not tell him how Hadley helped you siphon off a big chunk of every Double Bit check that went through his bank — ?"

"Ford — shut your mouth!"

"Why should I?" Tarrant asked. Wolffe had touched off a drunken panic in him and he couldn't stop. He seemed to be striking out at the man for past indignities, his voice wavering with a vindictive hysteria. "You've already spilled the beans. Overcharging Brian for everything he bought. Tell him about that. Pocketing the difference. The phony deposit slips and the false accounts and —"

With a curse Wolffe wheeled toward the man, swinging a vicious backhand blow at him. It caught Tarrant across the mouth and flung him heavily backward. He would have fallen if a post supporting the porch overhang hadn't been directly behind him; he sagged against it, grabbing the post to hold himself up. A rank hatred burned the drunken blaze from his eyes as he stared at Wolffe. He held a hand to his slack, bloody mouth and cursed foully.

Brian's mind was no longer blank. The surprise and shock were gone and the comprehension of Wolffe's full betrayal was beginning to move through him in a thin channel of sickness, growing rapidly to a tide, bitter and black.

Wolffe saw the expression on his face. Wolffe's anger at Tarrant faded from his black eyes; his broad shoulders sagged and there was a spent, drawn look about his mouth.

"Well," he said thinly, "you were bound to find out sooner or later."

Brian shook his head helplessly, still trying to grasp the reality of it. "What'd you want, George? You could have been rich off the retainer I paid you."

"Rich? Chicken-feed like that? What kind of man did you think I was? I licked boots long enough. I bowed and scraped and went without till I had my bellyfull. You didn't think I was going to stand by and see a fool throw away the biggest ranch in Arizona. What do you know about riches? You and Tarrant were the biggest men in the country, but you were pikers. You're going to see a different Double Bit come out of this." Wolffe's voice rose higher, a flush filled his face. "It'll be bigger than you could ever dream of!"

There was a feverish excitement in his face. It was like a revelation to Brian. The burning eyes, the covetous regard for money, the obsessive need to possess and maneuver and control.

Why hadn't he seen him like this before? He had merely indulged Wolffe, looking on him as a prudish older brother, knowing a certain fondness for him despite his faults.

"I guess I should have seen it a long time ago," he said.

Wolffe had subsided. He was breathing heavily, regaining his composure. "You wouldn't listen," he said.

"Tell me one thing, George. Did Arleen know what you were doing?"

"I never told her. Maybe she sensed it. I don't know." Wolffe stepped back onto the porch. "What's the difference?"

Brian looked at him. "Yeah," he said emptily. "What's the difference?"

17

Brian got back to Sandoval's near midnight. But the Yaqui was still waiting up for him. When Brian told him what had happened Sandoval began to pace around his little mud *jacal*.

"George Wolffe," he said. "George Wolffe."

"In a way you can't blame him," Brian said. "The kind of boyhood he had would twist anybody."

"Some men they want women. Some they want power. Is no explaining —" Sandoval stopped, turning to Brian, the question hanging between them.

Brian shook his head. "I'm convinced Asa didn't kill Cline."

"And the trial she's set for Saturday."

It maddened Brian to think he possessed the knowledge that might point the finger of guilt at Wolffe, yet had no proof that would stand up in court. That was Wolffe's strength; it was why he could admit to Brian what he had done and still know he was safe. And yet he had a weakness too. Knowing now that it had been Wolffe manipulating the strings from the beginning,

Brian could see how he had played one man off against the other till none of them trusted him. The seeds of distrust and hatred were already planted deep in Ford Tarrant. If they could be cultivated quickly enough — "What you think?" Sandoval asked.

"I'm thinking we still might have a chance to save Asa. What I heard this afternoon came out because Wolffe and Tarrant were at each other's throats. What if a man like Judge Parrish had heard it?"

"They wouldn't be fool enough to say anything in front of him."

"What if they didn't know he was there?"

"Brian, what you make?"

Brian rose restlessly, trying to piece together the fragments of a plan in his mind. It was only a vague idea yet. He poured himself a cup of coffee, bitter and black, frowning to himself.

"It may be a wild gamble, Chino, but it's all we have left to work with. Add it up this way. Do you remember how I was bushwacked in Skeleton Canyon that time I went out to tell the Gillettes they could stay on their land?"

Chino nodded. "You told us."

"Wolffe must have set that up. He thought the Salt Rivers would fold if Gillette pulled out. And he thought Pa would quit if I foreclosed."

"So he make it look like the Gillettes they try to kill you. Then he sure you foreclose."

"Right. And now Cline is killed under similar circumstances."

"Wolffe again?"

"I'm convinced of it. And it makes sort of a pattern, doesn't it?" Brian sipped at the coffee, frowning. Somehow he had to get Wolffe and Tarrant together again. The Double Bit was out of the question. There would be too many hands around. And Apache Wells would be no good. He remembered that more than once, when going into town, he and Tarrant had met at the old Archuleta place. It was the halfway point between the two ranches. He said, "Suppose Tarrant got a note from Wolffe, asking him to meet Wolffe at the Archuleta ruins. Tarrant would have to come through Skeleton Canyon. And suppose he was bushwacked there."

A bright glow came to Chino's eyes, as he recognized the implications. Then he shook his head. "How you know Wolffe write that letter?"

"I'll do it for him, Chino. While I practice my handwriting, you get Wirt Peters."

For twenty years Brian had known George Wolffe's strong, deeply slanted handwriting: yet he still practiced an hour after Chino left before he was satisfied. The first letter was to Ford Tarrant:

Ford: —

I must see you immediately. Brian's told Judge Parrish what he heard yesterday, though he has no proof to back it up. We've got to establish an airtight alibi for our whereabouts during the time of Cline's murder, and we've got to be sure not to

240

get our lines crossed. The Double Bit is no place to meet now. The Archuleta ruins would be better. I'll be waiting there at moonrise.

George

The second note Brian addressed to himself:

Brian: —

I can understand your anger at finding out I was the one who engineered everything. But you'll recall we always wanted to let you sit in. And what you said in Apache Wells convinces me that you realize how hopeless the fight has become, and that you're ready to come back to your own people. Ford is our weak link. I've tried to ease him out, but he still has the power to checkmate me. With a Sheridan back at the Double Bit, Ford would be nothing on the Rim. So I'm willing to make a bargain. Agree to come back and I'll give you proof that will save Asa. If you'll meet me at the Archuleta place about moonrise tonight, I'll have it with me.

George

He wondered how Tarrant would look when he showed it to him.

Near dawn, Sandoval returned with Wirt Peters. Brian was certain of Peters's loyalty now. But the man had once worked for Tarrant and they had put pressure on him from the beginning to rejoin the Tarrant faction. For Peters to make the move now would seem logical, with the Salt

Rivers facing certain and final defeat over Cline's murder. Peters agreed to take the letter, supposedly from Wolffe, to Tarrant. He would tell Tarrant that Wolffe had persuaded him to come over to their side.

It would take Peters most of the morning to reach Tarrant, and that gave Brian time for his next step. Rousing Pancho, he ate a hurried breakfast and went to saddle up. Both Sandoval and Brian were groggy from the sleepless night. Slinging a Mexican-tree saddle aboard the extra horse they were taking for Judge Parrish, Sandoval emitted a prodigious yawn.

"This ain't going to be so easy. That Wolffe he's a smarter one than Ford Tarrant."

"Not so smart when he's mad," Brian said. "We've got to get him to the old Archuleta place on time, and weve got to have him so hopping mad he's ready to jump down Ford's throat."

Sandoval didn't press it. Brian had given him a hint last night of what he had in mind.

All the way into Apache Wells Brian was thinking about it. About Arleen. That was the part he hated. If he could have gotten to Wolffe any other way, he would have done so. But time was short and he had to use the only weapon left.

It involved his relationship with Arleen. The question he still couldn't answer. But what he'd learned at the Double Bit yesterday threw new light on it. Wolffe hadn't told Arleen what he was doing to Brian. But maybe she had sensed it. That was how Wolffe put it.

And if she sensed it, why hadn't she told Brian? Loyalty to her brother? Then how strong did that leave her love for Brian?

It was noon when they reached town. The crowd was gone from in front of the jail and through the open door a deputy was visible dozing at the desk. Wolffe's buckboard was not parked in the alley below his office. That meant he was still at the Double Bit, as Brian had figured. They rode into the alley and Brian dismounted, looking up at the windows. He thought of all the times he had come here, of the laughter and the comradeship and the passion.

"Chino," he said. "It's a dirty world."

Sandoval did not answer. Brian started up the rickety stairs. He stopped at the door, staring blankly at it, reluctance lying upon him like a weight. Finally he knocked. He heard her light step inside, and the door opened.

She wore a dress of watered blue silk with a vivid red sash about her waist. Her black hair was pulled plum-tight against her head, shimmering like wet silk in the light, and a pair of copper earrings lent her face a barbaric touch. She started to smile, then let it fade. She didn't bother to hide her confusion. Her lips were parted, damp and red. Her voice sounded a little breathless.

"I hardly expected —" she said.

"I know." He took off his hat and tried to smile.

She stepped back and allowed him to enter.

243

The door made a soft click at his side. He looked around at the familiar furniture, the frilly curtains. Her skirt rustled softly as she moved around him. Once he had wanted this woman more than anything else in the world. How could you wipe out such a desire?

She stood before him. He spoke quickly. "We sparred before, Arleen. We beat around the bush and we were afraid and we lost it somehow. Let's not lose it again."

She shook her head, puzzled. "Brian —"

"You said it would take time. You were right. But now we've had the time. I know where I stand for good. The Salt Rivers are through. I never belonged with them anyway. I'm clearing out. But I'm not going with empty pockets."

"Brian, what's happened?"

"Nothing yet. But I've got a chance to get back part of what I lost. Let's be honest. Your brother was behind it all. Tarrant was just a figurehead."

A stricken look came to her face. She bit her lip and turned away, walking to the window. He followed.

"You knew. Admit it."

"Not for sure. I just had a feeling — I —"

"That was the thing between us — the barrier. Those strange moods the year before it happened. Not being able to answer when I asked you to marry me."

She nodded helplessly.

For a moment he felt like hell. She couldn't be that good an actress. She was really miserable.

He took her shoulders in his hands. They were like satin, burning against his palms.

"I don't blame you. They had you on the rack. How could you expose George when you didn't know for sure?"

She turned, tears in her eyes, torture. She looked into his face as if searching for understanding, sympathy, forgiveness. It was all there and for a moment what he was doing gagged him.

"Arleen —" He could hardly make it. "The cards are on the table. That's in the past now. All that matters is you and me. Knowing for certain that George did, you can't feel any loyalty to him now."

She hesitated a moment, then lowered her head, shaking it miserably from side to side.

"We've got to fight for our chance," he said. "There's a way to get some of it back."

Slowly her head raised. "A way?"

"Tarrant's meeting me at the Archuleta place tonight. He's got something that'll blow the whole thing sky high. All we need is some of those deposit slips George was using when he was juggling my accounts."

She pulled back. "George —"

"He was willing to ruin everything for us, wasn't he?"

She bit her lip, not answering. With a soft curse he released her and walked to the desk. Before he could open the first drawer she spoke, "It's no use."

He looked up. "Are they at the Double Bit?"

She shook her head. "Brian . . . don't ask me . . . my own brother."

He walked back to her. His tall figure threw a dark shadow across her face and his red hair blazed like an angry god's in the lamplight.

"How can you go on defending George, knowing for certain what he did to me?"

She wouldn't meet his eyes. She was looking at his chest. A little muscle twitched in her cheek. He was staring at the cameo of her face, trying to see how much was sincere reaction, how much was synthetic. He couldn't tell. He felt like a heel and yet it had to go on, he couldn't stop now, with Asa's life at stake.

He said her name and he took her in his arms and kissed her. It was hard, savage, bruising. The reaction ran through her whole body. She moaned and arched herself against him and locked her arms about his neck. He could feel her tremble and at least that wasn't synthetic. He had drawn out the old passion, more vivid, more urgent than he'd ever seen it in her before.

In that first moment the animal in him couldn't help but respond to the hot length of her whole body glued to his. Then it was gone. Heat was gone and desire was gone and there was the taste of ashes in his mouth. It was the answer he had looked for ever since Estelle had asked him. In a single instant all the doubt and confusion was swept from him and he knew.

He let Arleen's response run its course and

when she pulled back he was a prisoner who had been freed. She was breathing heavily, deeply shaken. Her eyes were wide and startled and as she looked at him he saw the same dazed wonder he had seen in Latigo when the man finally realized Brian had whipped him.

"You and me," he said. "It was never meant to be any different, was it?"

Her lips moved faintly. "Brian, I only wish —"

He grasped her shoulders. "George is your brother, sure — but now it's up to you to choose between us." Holding her gaze, he let his voice go hard. "I'll meet you at the Archuleta place about ten. It'll give you time to get the deposit slips. I'll see you there."

"Of course, Brian. I'll be there."

Her suddenly brittle tone gave Brian the certain feeling that Wolffe, not she, would show up at Archuleta's. His whole plan depended on it.

18

Outside he stood with his back against the closed door for a moment. He was trembling now in reaction, feeling none of the savagery or strength he'd shown Arleen. Finally he went down to the men waiting in the alley.

"You do it?" Pancho asked.

Brian mounted his horse. "I don't know."

"How about her?" Sandoval asked.

"What the hell," Brian said angrily. "It's been a gamble from the beginning, hasn't it?" He saw Sandoval react and was immediately sorry. He was edgy as a skittish bronc after what he'd been through. He slapped Sandoval's shoulder. "Don't pay any attention to me. Let's go get the judge."

They rode up back alleys to the Cochise Hotel, where Judge Parrish was staying. While Pancho held the extra horse and their two animals, Brian and Sandoval went up the back stairs to Parrish's room. They knocked and in a moment Parrish answered. He wore his bathrobe and slippers and held a brief in his hand. Lamplight made a snowy nimbus of his white hair.

"We've got some evidence we'd like you to hear, Judge," Brian said. "Out at the Archuleta place."

The man's patrician face narrowed disapprovingly. "Can't you present it here?"

"We haven't got time to explain. It might mean a man's life."

Parrish had an orator's voice. "Gentlemen, I've got a dozen briefs to review before Saturday. I can't ride all over the desert on some fantastic hoax —"

Brian touched his gun. "Don't make us use force."

Rage made a pale ridge about the judge's lips "Abduction. Threatening the court. Contempt. Twenty years, gentlemen, and I'll be glad to pass the sentence myself."

"In the meantime," Brian said, "do you want to come with us on your feet, or hanging over a horse on your belly?"

Parrish looked at the gun, at their grim, dust-grimed faces. With a hopeless curse he turned back inside; they followed and waited for him to dress, then accompanied him downstairs to the waiting horses. They left town by back alleys and turned northward into the broken land that tumbled down off the Rim.

As they rode, they told Judge Parrish what they knew, what they suspected, and what they planned. It simmered him down somewhat, but he still thought the whole thing fantastic. They followed an old Indian trail through the broken, lifting country until they reached a fork. The right branch led to the Archuleta place; the left one twisted into higher country and eventually entered Skeleton Canyon.

"If I'm figuring right," Brian told Sandoval, "you and the judge will reach the Archuleta place ahead of everybody else. Try and get into that old wine cellar off the patio. You can hear from there and you won't be seen."

Sandoval seemed about to speak. Then he thought better of it, gave Brian a tight grin, an affectionate punch on the shoulder, and turned to edge the judge off onto the right fork. Fuming and fretting, Parrish preceded the Yaqui into the brush. Brian glanced at Pancho, then led him onto the left branch. It was late afternoon and the clouds were flying ragged crimson banners above the broken silhouette of the Rim when they reached the yawning mouth of the canyon. They penetrated it half a mile to the trail Tarrant would use coming down into the canyon; if Brian was traveling from Sandoval's to the Archuleta ruins, this was the point where he and Tarrant would most logically meet. Brian and Pancho dismounted and sought fresh tracks, without success. Brian knew it would have taken Wirt Peters most of the morning to reach Tarrant's and it would take Tarrant another three or four hours to reach this point in the canyon.

"Looks like I timed it right," Brian told Pancho. "If Ford fell for the note, he's still coming." He squinted his eyes at rimrock and lifted a hand toward the castellated heights. "Get up there with your gun. When he shows, let him catch up with me. Then start shooting. Get as close as you can without hitting."

Pancho wiped the back of his hand across a sweating brow. "You sure you know what you do, *amigo?*"

Brian gave him a bleak grin. "I want hell scared out of him, Pancho. I'd do it with your face but he might have heart failure."

The Mexican laughed gustily. "*Hombre,* how can you make a man laugh at his own insult?"

He kicked his scrawny bronc up the switch-backs to rimrock and Brian pulled into the shadows shrouding the canyon. The moment of humor passed and the strain of tension began to set in. He had showed Pancho a confidence he didn't feel. Could he really be certain of his own timing? Or maybe Tarrant hadn't fallen for the note. And what if he took a different trail?

He tried to shake the apprehensions off. This was the only logical route to the ruins. And Brian knew the rotten core of the man now. Fear of being involved in Cline's murder should send him scurrying like a rat to Wolffe.

He had been waiting in the shade half an hour when he saw furtive motion on the rimrock. Sunlight flashed against metal and he knew Pancho was signaling him. He turned his horse into the canyon, heading westward. He moved slowly, rounding one turn, another. He was out of sight of the trail but he could hear the faint rattle of a horse coming down off the switchbacks into the floor of the canyon; the scraping echo of hoofs on shale grew louder and a rider rounded the nearest turn behind. He looked back and saw Ford Tarrant. The man's handsome bottle-green frock coat was powdered with dust.

He almost pulled his horse to a halt, at sight of Brian. Then, wary as a strange dog, he let the animal walk forward.

"You spend a lot of time in enemy country," he said.

Brian smiled enigmatically. "Maybe I like the view."

Tarrant stopped three feet away, suspicion muddying his eyes. "You aren't going to see Wolffe again?"

Brian still smiled. "After what I found out yesterday?"

Reaction ran through Tarrant's face and he started to speak. The first gunshot drowned his voice. Brian saw the slug kick up a miniature fountain of dust and shale ten feet ahead of them. The shooting sound made the horses squeal and rear. Tarrant's animal bolted before he could check it. The echoes of that first shot crashed back and forth between the canyon walls, a deafening bedlam of sound. It obliterated the second shot, but Tarrant's running horse was only a dozen yards ahead of Brian when he saw it jerk, leap into the air, and flop over on its side like a great fish. Its flailing legs struck the ground and that pitched Tarrant from the saddle, to be lost in the cloud of dirt plowed up by the sliding, falling animal.

Brian let his own frightened horse run past them and when he saw a sandy spot he pulled up on the animal, causing it to rear, and took a dive as though he had been pitched off. He hit on a shoulder in the soft sand, flopping against a mat of creosote brush.

The echoes of gunfire still filled the gorge. He saw Tarrant, with his gun out, squirming to the cover of rocks. Brian pulled his gun and crawled toward the man, shooting upward into the air as though returning fire. A bullet struck granite a foot from Tarrant, screaming off in ricochet. The noise was deafening. Brian reached Tarrant, huddling behind the rock with him. Panic turned Tarrant's face slack and foolish. Fright shimmered in his eyes as he fired wildly at the unseen gunman above.

Another slug struck close, howling off the rock in ricochet. Tarrant jerked back into cover. "Brian," he shouted. His voice was shrill, cracked. "What the hell! Do something —"

Brian made another show of returning fire, wincing as a ricochet whined too close for comfort, adding to the bedlam with the crashing racket of his own gun, firing till it was empty and then sprawling back into the sand beside the man. The echoes rolled down into the gorge and died reluctantly against the distant sounding boards of unseen cliffs. The silence crept against the men like a furtive pressure, an ache in the ears after so much awesome noise.

Brian thumbed a pair of shells into his gun and glanced tentatively at the rimrock. He drew no fire. They lay against the rocks, sweating, trying to see movement on the heights, until enough time had elapsed to convince Tarrant they were safe.

"I guess that's it," Brian said. He looked at Tarrant's horse, lying dead down the canyon. He knew Pancho hadn't meant to hit the animal, but it made things more convincing. "Lucky you got pitched," he said. "If you'd been in the saddle another ten feet it would've been you instead of the horse."

A pallor stole the ruddiness from Tarrant's cheeks. "Have they gone crazy?" he asked.

"Who?"

"The Salt Rivers."

Brian let a look of disgust come to his face. "Don't try to cover up, Ford."

The man gaped blankly. "What?"

"The Salt Rivers wouldn't shoot at me. What happened? Did you and Wolffe get your wires crossed somehow?"

Tarrant's eyes widened; then he shook his head. "Brian, I had nothing to do with —"

"Maybe you figured I heard too much yesterday."

"Brian, I swear —"

"I suppose you don't even know about this."

Brian yanked out the letter he had written to himself, dropping it contemptuously at the man's hand. Still sprawled against the rock, Tarrant opened it wonderingly. Surprise, fear, rage — they all shuttled through his face as he read.

Brian frowned at him. "You knew about it," he said accusingly.

Exasperatedly Ford pulled out the note Brian had written him. Brian took it and made a pretense of reading, letting confusion replace the bitter accusation in his face. Finally, softly, he said, "So that's it. After yesterday we both know enough to hang him."

Tarrant shook his head helplessly, suspicion and fear still mingled in his face.

"You still think it was the Salt Rivers?" Brian asked.

"He wouldn't," Tarrant said doggedly. "He couldn't —"

"There's one way to find out," Brian said. "If he really wanted us to reach the Archuleta place, he'd be there." Brian felt on safe ground in saying this. If Wolffe was at Archuleta's — and he had to be — he'd be in hiding when Tarrant and Brian showed up, waiting to hear what they had to say. And once Tarrant was convinced Wolffe had tried to bushwack him, nothing Wolffe said would change his mind.

Tarrant glanced at him sharply, speculatively, then looked out at his dead horse. Brian could see that the man was still bitterly confused, not completely convinced. Yet the wording of the note Wolffe had purportedly written to Brian had planted a deep suspicion in Tarrant's mind; and the apparent attempt to kill him should, Brian figured, shock him into a showdown with Wolffe. Finally, in a husky voice, he said:

"How'll we get there?"

"Well," Brian said, "I never thought I'd ride double with a snake."

It took them half an hour to find Brian's horse, where it had spooked down the canyon. Then, through the mauve haze of late afternoon, through the long twilight of the desert evening, they made their way out of the canyon and along the tumbled country edging the Rim to the Archuleta place.

They came upon it after dark, an ancient Spanish colonial rancho built in this land a hundred years before the Yankees came, its deserted and crumbling buildings overlooked on all sides by the towering buttes and weirdly eroded mesa of the dropoff just below the Rim. Brian pulled the horse to a halt in the shelter of a dense mesquite thicket, looking intently at the silent buildings.

If Arleen had gone to the Double Bit as soon as Brian left her, she would have reached her brother by afternoon. And if Wolffe had acted immediately on her information, he should have reached the Archuleta ruins by now.

"I don't see anybody," Tarrant said.

"We'd better make sure," Brian said.

He lifted the reins and the weary horse moved at a jaded walk into the weed-grown yard. The house had been built in the typical style of colonial Spain, the fort-like walls protecting it from the marauding Indians of an earlier age, the outside rooms built around a central patio. In most places the roof had fallen, its heavy beams broken or tilting crazily toward the sky. The walls were crumbling and a dozen breaches yawned darkly, opening into the shadowy interior.

Brian rode the horse boldly through one of the openings and into the main *sala,* the cavernous living-room that ran across the front of the house. He guided the animal through heaps of rubble and fallen beams, across a stretch of comparatively open floor, and stopped at the narrow hallway leading into the central patio. They dismounted and ground-hitched the horse and moved cautiously through the pitch-black hall and into the patio. The moon was beginning to rise, casting its eerie light into the weed-covered enclosure that was surrounded on all sides by the house.

In one corner, half-hidden by a heap of rubble, were the stairs leading to the wine cellar. If Parrish and Sandoval had gotten here first, they would be in that dank cavern now, waiting, listening.

And if Wolffe had come later, undoubtedly with Latigo, they would be in one of the bedrooms on the north side, or perhaps in the kitchen at the rear.

Brian glanced around, prodded by the pressures of tension, doubt, possible error. Had he misjudged Arleen? He was so sure he'd found the answer today. It was Arleen's primary allegiance that had held her to her brother before. It had to mold her now.

Tarrant came into the patio behind Brian, nervous, looking quickly around. The rattle of his boots against the rubble was the only sound.

"Nobody's here," he said.

The brittle, shaking tone of his voice told Brian a lot. The man was becoming increasingly convinced that the notes had been lures, that Wolffe had tried to kill them both in Skeleton Canyon. He was enraged and panicked by the thought, ready to jump in any direction.

If Wolffe was listening, the talk would have to sound as though this were a prearranged meeting. Yet Brian had to draw something out of Tarrant that would sound like a betrayal of Wolffe. He began ambiguously.

"We might as well face it, Ford. We're in the same boat."

Tarrant paced in a little circle, lips white at the edges. "Damn him, *damn* him . . ."

"I guess those deposit slips drove him against the wall. Once the court sees those the whole thing will snowball."

Tarrant's eyes popped. "Deposit slips?"

Brian smiled enigmatically. "You didn't think I was bluffing yesterday when I said I had proof of Asa's innocence, did you? Why else would Wolffe be so jumpy? It's piling up against him. One word from you could pin him down. Cline's murder and all."

Tarrant moistened his lips. "You haven't got proof on that."

Brian knew he had to risk a guess now. But it was a logical guess, since Tarrant had worked so closely with Wolffe up to now. "We know now you were there when Wolffe planned the killing, though I thought till yesterday afternoon it was you who planned it. But they hang accessories too, Ford."

The man's beefy jowls quivered. "I was against it. I told him he was going too far —"

He stopped short as he realized his admission. Brian showed little reaction, smiling thinly. "Never mind. You're not telling us anything new. It's yourself you've got to protect now. A man can turn state's evidence, make a bargain with the court. Tell what you know and it might even get you off clean."

"State's evidence." Tarrant said it softly, scowling thoughtfully. Brian could almost see the possibilities working their way into his rotten core. He was in something too big and too dangerous for him to cope with. It had started out with a little political juggling and had ended with murder. And now his own life was threatened. He was a man in deep water, willing to reach for any straw that might pull him out.

Brian heard his horse whinny and stir fretfully

inside the house. Were they moving in? It sent a ripple of tension through him. He heard a faint scrape from the hall and covered it quickly with his voice.

"You've got to jump first, Ford. We can't give him a chance to try again."

Ford moistened his lips, nodded furtively. "You're right."

"Shall we see Judge Parrish?"

Tarrant glanced sharply at him, face pale and stiff. The suggestion was too final, and Brian could see him begin to recoil.

"It's either you or Wolffe now, Ford. Are you going to give him a chance to try again?"

Memory of Skeleton Canyon sent another little spasm through Tarrant's florid face and he shook his head. "No. You're right. It's me or him."

He turned involuntarily toward the house. Then he stopped, with a husky sound of surprise. George Wolffe stood in one of the gaps in the wall. The brim of his flat-topped hat dropped a black slice of shadow across his broad face. He held a six-shooter in his hand. A sick letdown came to Brian. He knew he should feel triumph. But now he realized he hadn't wanted to be right about Arleen; hadn't wanted this proof of the taint in her.

The tails of Wolffe's clawhammer coat whispered against his shanks as he moved into the moonlit patio. Brian waited for Latigo to appear. He didn't think Wolffe would have come alone.

"So that's what you'd blow the lid off with," Wolffe said to Tarrant. "State's evidence."

"Why shouldn't he?" Brian said. And still no Latigo. "You were ready to throw him to the wolves. And you've been doing it to me from the beginning. No wonder you wanted me to settle down, I was spending too much of the money you figured was yours."

Wolffe frowned at Tarrant. "You haven't been listening to this man?"

"Why not?" Tarrant said. His voice was shrill, outraged. "After Latigo tried to cut me down in Skeleton Canyon!"

"The same way he cut down Cline," Brian said. "You must have been real anxious to see that Latigo did as efficient a job this time, George. Otherwise you wouldn't still be here."

"That's a filthy lie. Everybody knows Asa killed Cline," Wolffe said sharply.

Tarrant shook his head. "It's no use, George. They know the whole thing. How you planned it, who was there, everything."

Wolffe's face turned pale in reaction. Then a feral glow lit his eyes. He lifted his gun, swinging it toward Brian, cocking it. "Then maybe you know too much."

Sandoval moved from behind the rubble heap hiding the cellar stairs. "Drop the gun, Wolffe."

Wolffe wheeled involuntarily toward the Yaqui.

Brian called, "Chino — watch out — Latigo —"

He was pulling his own six-shooter as he yelled. Before he had finished a gun blasted from one of the window's on the north side. Sandoval was hit, staggering backward. Wolffe tried to whirl back to Brian. Brian fired. Wolffe jerked, took a step backward, then fell forward onto his hands and knees. Brian was already plunging for the protection of the hall door. The second shot from the north window smashed adobe off the wall inches behind him as he plunged into the hall.

He heard the dim pound of boots through the north bedrooms. He knew it was Latigo now and guessed the man was trying to reach the main *sala* first, thus trapping Brian in the narrow hall. Brian took a chance on his head start and ran headlong in to the cavernous living-room. He almost crashed into the horse, ground-hitched by the hall door. The animal squealed in fright and jumped a few feet down the wall toward the north end of the room.

At at the same time Latigo plunged from the bedroom doorway at that end. Even as he came out he realized he had lost the race, and checked his headlong run to dodge back into cover. Brian's snap shot slammed into the sagging door an instant after the man had disappeared.

Brian flattened himself against the wall. The nearest cover was the fallen beams and rubble heaps in the center of the room. They were fifteen feet away and Brian could not gain them without exposing himself to Latigo's fire. Flattened against the wall, he heard a dragging sound behind him, like a bale of hay pulled across the floor. He grew rigid against the wall, trying to identify the sound. Then he remembered Wolffe, going to his hands and knees in the patio. That was all it could be. Wolffe, wounded, on his hands and knees, crawling, dragging himself through the hall toward the *sala,* intent on getting Brian before his life leaked out of him.

It bracketed Brian. He was between the two doorways, his back against the wall. Whichever man he turned to meet, it would expose his back to the other. The sweat on his face turned icy. His mouth went dry as cotton and his eyes swept the room vainly for a way out. Only a couple of seconds left. With that insistent, dragging sound growing louder all the time.

Then the horse shifted nervously, ten feet down the wall toward Latigo. The shots had spooked the animal and it was fiddling and snorting. Brian saw his chance. He ran toward the horse, keeping it between him and the bedroom door.

He slapped the animal's rump with all his strength. The horse squealed and bolted. Brian caught a stirrup leather with his left hand, running on its off side so the horse would be between him and Latigo as they passed the bedroom door. Running headlong, the horse almost dragging him off his feet, he was suddenly opposite the black maw of the bedroom door.

He had a shadowy glimpse of Latigo's surprised movement. The man gave a wild shout and fired in panic, probably still not understanding what had happened. The bullet chewed leather from the cantle of the saddle and whined past Brian's head. He released the stirrup leather, firing over the horse's rump at Latigo's gun-flash.

He fired twice more as the horse ran from between him and the door. The horse galloped out through a breach in the wall and the echoes of its passage and of the gunfire died swiftly. Brian was left in a void of stillness.

There was no movement from the bedroom door, no sound. Then George Wolffe crawled out of the hall. Brian wheeled toward the man. Wolffe's gun lay against the floor, gripped in a hand that was smeared with blood. He looked at Brian with glassy eyes. Crouched on hands and knees, he tried to lift his gun.

"You know too much, Brian . . ."

Blood bubbled from his mouth. He hung that way, gun half lifted. Then his eyes rolled up in his head and he sagged full length on the floor. Brian gazed emptily at the man a moment. No feeling would come, no reaction. Like an automaton he moved into the bedroom to check Latigo. The foreman lay on his back. Two bullets had struck his chest and he was dead. Brian walked back into the main *sala*. A thin nausea was beginning to move through him now. Pancho called from somewhere outside the house and Brian answered. In another moment the man appeared, looking at Wolffe with round eyes.

"Dios," he said. "I wish I followed you closer. I could help."

"You did your job," Brian said. He felt drained now, apathetic, sick. Sandoval stumbled into the room, holding a shattered arm. Brian went quickly to him, pulling his bandanna off.

"Don't treat me like the baby," Sandoval grunted. "She's just little nick."

Judge Parrish moved testily out of the hall, prodding Tarrant ahead of him with a drawn gun. He looked down at Wolffe and shook his white head. "Damnedest court I ever held. But what I heard tonight will sure free Asa. If you get another judge to sit on the case I'll be a witness to this whole thing."

"You can't prove anything," Tarrant said sullenly.

"You said enough tonight to convict you of complicity in Cline's murder," Judge Parrish told the man. "The only hope you have is in state's evidence. Tell the whole thing and it might get you some leniency."

Tarrant didn't answer. But Brian knew there was little core to the man. "I think he'll talk," Brian said. "Can you ride with that wound, Chino?"

"Sure," the Yaqui said. He grinned at Brian.

It was long after midnight when they reached Apache Wells. Brian was surprised to see a light still burning in the rooms Estelle and Cameron had taken at the hotel. Parrish and Pancho told Brian they would take care of Tarrant, freeing Brian to go to the hotel. It was a long time before Estelle answered the door. She was still dressed and her eyes, heavy and half-closed with sleep, made her look like a little girl.

"I guess I went to sleep in the chair," she said. "I —"

The look on his face stopped her. She moved back and he stepped into the room, telling her in a rush what had happened. It brought her wide awake and when she learned Asa was cleared she almost cried with relief and happiness.

"I guess we've all won," she said. "Surely you can get part of the Double Bit back, with this proof of what Wolffe did."

It surprised him that he hadn't thought of that yet. It made him realize how little that mattered now in comparison with the other things he had found during these last months. She seemed to sense the direction of his thoughts and didn't press it. Already the expression of her face was changing. She seemed to be searching for something in his eyes. He knew what it was. There remained but one question to be answered.

"That's over too, Estelle. Arleen doesn't have any more hold on me."

They both hesitated a moment longer, looking at each other, on the brink of something as they had been so often before. But now there was nothing to hold them back. He touched her and then he took her in his arms and kissed her. He felt the warm tears on her cheeks and she buried her face against his chest. He held her tight.

"It's all over now," he said. "It's all over."

"No it isn't," she whispered. "It's just begun."

W